# THREE WAYS *of* THE SAW

*Stories*

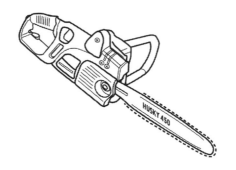
HUSKY 450

# THREE WAYS *of* THE SAW

*Stories*

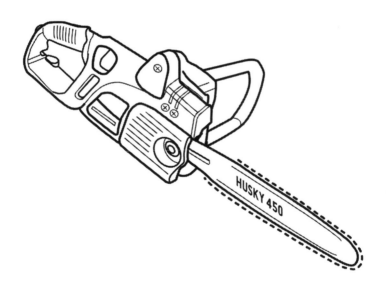

HUSKY 450

# Matt Mullins

An Atticus Trade Paperback Original

Atticus Books LLC
3766 Howard Avenue, Suite 202
Kensington MD 20895
http://atticusbooksonline.com

Some stories from *Three Ways of the Saw*, many in slightly
altered form, first appeared in *decomP, Hobart, Hunger
Mountain, Mid American Review, Pleiades, subTerrain, Ugly
Accent, Umbrella, Many Mountains Moving*, and *The Grand
Valley Review*.

ISBN-13: 978-0-9832080-6-8
ISBN-10: 0-9832080-6-9

Typeset in Sabon
Cover design by Jamie Keenan

## Acknowledgements

Thank you to:

My father, for his advice and encouragement.

My mother and sisters, for their love and belief.

Those friends, here and gone, whose influence had a hand in these stories.

# Table of Contents

For Megan and Nola June

# I

# BLACK SHEEP MISSIVES

*When the skull plates close*
*when the squinting navel*
*forgets its roots, all who bear*
*the mark of birth will hear a cry in the night,*
*and a child will sit up, amazed*
*in the crib of bones.*

John Woods, "Birthmark"


*That is why in the distance you see*
*beyond the first ridge of low hills*
*where nothing ever grows, men and women*
*astride mules, on horseback, some even*
*on foot, all the lost family you*
*never prayed to see, praying to see you,*
*chanting and singing to bring the moon*
*down into the last of the sunlight.*

Philip Levine, "Ask for Nothing"

# Dead Falls

It's a shaky, hand-held, Super 8 memory, overexposed in washed-out color, a scene from the seventies where everything seems to burn with a white light from within. Some parts are in slow motion, other parts are fast and jerky, but it's always just the two of us, me and my best friend Ted, taking showers after a summer day of playing army and wrestling and stealing small toys and candy from the dime store.

Ted lived a few houses down my street, and it seemed we'd always been best friends, even though we were nothing alike. He wasn't shy and self-conscious like me, but confident and popular and better at everything I wished I could do well. He was clean-limbed, summer-tanned Ted, the fastest kid in our seventh grade class at the fifty yard dash, the only one who took the rope climb too far during gym, past the red flag to tag the iron beam the rope itself was tied around. It was Ted who I let cheat over my shoulder because I had the grades. It was Ted who made a balance beam out of the high brick wall that surrounded the hospital parking lot. So when Ted suggested we shower off the day's dirt together to give us more time to play before his mom made us dinner, I followed his lead.

We showered quickly, ignoring soap like boys will. Afterwards, we drew with our fingers on the fogged-up bathroom mirror. I wrote the words *dumb fuck*, something I'd recently been called by an eighth-grader after bumping into him in the hallway. Ted made the outline of a dick with balls then put a circle around it and added some eyes to make a dick-nose face, which we laughed at before he wiped it away with his towel.

"Lay down on your back and close your eyes," he said.

"No way," I said.

"I dare you."

Ted had accepted, without hesitation, every single dare I'd ever put to him in all the years we'd been friends. On top of that, he'd thought up stunts I couldn't even begin to imagine: chewing up living bumblebees, spray painting *PORK* on the side of a parked cop car, sticking an M-80 into someone's mailbox on a day when we knew a paycheck was inside. Once, I watched him lift his father's wallet off the kitchen island and slip out a twenty-dollar bill with his mother doing dishes not three feet away. He waved the money at her back and winked at me before shoving it into the pocket of his jeans.

"Okay, but I get to dare you next," I said.

I cinched my towel tighter around my waist and took my suspicions with me down to the bathroom floor. We'd been around each other naked in the locker room after gym class enough times; I had ideas about what was coming: an Indian burn twisting into my arm, the snapped sting of a rat-tailed towel on my stomach, shampoo up my nose.

"Quit being such a pussy and close your eyes," Ted said.

My tingling skin was set on edge. A touch: hard, soft, ticklish, sharp, could come at me from anywhere at any time. Everything was still for much too long. I started wondering if he'd somehow snuck, ninja-like, out of the bathroom without my hearing. That was the kind of thing Ted could do, move in perfect silence, open a door and slip through, then shut it behind him without making a sound, somehow even keeping the latch from clicking. Then my wondering turned to something else as I felt the pulse of his breath on my bare chest and the heat of his skin close to mine.

"Open your mouth," he said.

I shook my head. This wasn't a dare to hop on one foot along the top of the hospital parking lot wall or give some high school kid the finger or steal a *Playboy* magazine or a 100 Grand Bar. We weren't in a locker room full of seventh-graders talking shit and making fun of each other's fuzz. I tried to remember a single time I'd told Ted no. I couldn't think of one. Palms pressed against the sweaty tiles, I searched for answers in the Braille of grout. I found nothing but straight lines that kept turning in right angles back upon themselves.

"Wuss," Ted said. "C'mon. I double dare you."

I have never had many close friends, and Ted was the best friend of the few I had back then. It wasn't too difficult to convince myself we were just fucking with each other like always. A gob of shaving cream or a squeeze of toothpaste. A couple squirts from the hand soap dispenser or the shampoo bottle. Whatever he put in my mouth I could rinse out in the end. Then it would be my turn.

I opened wide. His hands slapped the floor past my head. The air around my face stirred slightly as his toenail scratched my leg. I felt him hovering above me, ready to drop onto my head and squeeze my skull in a scissor lock like he did when we were wrestling. A drip of water splashed against my lip. Something grazed my tooth. Then his presence fell away, and I heard him laughing. When I snapped my eyes open, Ted covered them with his hand.

"Hey," I said, half sitting up as he pushed me back down, "It's my turn now."

"No. Keep 'em closed. Dare ain't over."

My heart pounded. Jangling nerves had me light-headed and leaden at once. I could sense him moving around, getting closer. His ankles knocked against my toweled hipbones.

"Okay, sit up."

Ready to be done with it all, I sat up, straight into a musky dampness. I opened my eyes to find I had just put my nose right into the crack of his ass.

"You fucker!" I shoved him away hard enough to bounce his head off the door.

Curled up on the floor rubbing the top of his skull, he laughed at me between groans.

"Oh man," he said, "If only you knew what else I did."

"What did you do? Tell me what you did!"

"You know."

I did know, or at least I had a pretty good idea, and what unsettled me was trying to understand why I hadn't stopped him, why I always let him tell me what to do. But we were just goofing around, weren't we? Or were we gay? Or was it only him who was gay? Or just me? And what did any of that mean when gay was a word Ted and me only used to describe stuff we thought was boring or stupid? I didn't have those answers, just like I didn't know if the ache in my chest was caused by anger or desire. Sure, anything from a schoolbook in my lap to sleeping on my stomach had been giving me a hard on lately, but why did I feel a stirring beneath my towel when I spent nights tracing in my mind the curve of Suzie Maselle's breasts?

Until then it had been one of our typical summer days. We'd ridden our bikes around the neighborhood, looking for ways to kill the time. We poked sticks at a flattened cat and checked people's mailboxes for magazines to steal. We rode to the mall and acted obnoxious in the Hudson's lingerie department until they kicked us out. We shoplifted model army men from the hobby store for our dioramas and got away with it. Finally, we ended up like we often did, doing dead falls among the curving brick walls near the hospital parking lot entrance. I thought back to our trampling the carefully landscaped bushes and lawns as we screamed imaginary bullets at each other ("BRATTA-TATTA-TATT!") then took turns twisting ourselves into these spastic, exaggerated tumbles that ended with us falling to the ground and flopping like landed fish into a final stillness from which we would jump up laughing.

Now I felt like he'd just shot at me for real. I didn't know whether I wanted to leave right then or stay and help him sneak a cup of gas after dinner so we could go behind the garage and burn into wads of melted plastic the model tanks and planes we were constantly building. There were two sides of me pointing guns at each other, and all these bullets of feeling were turning through my guts as I stood and tried to understand what it would mean if I stayed. What it would mean if I left.

Ted's laughter trailed off as he sat up and leaned back against the bathroom door.

"Your turn," he said.

He had me. For all I knew, this was a genuine invitation to do something similar, something he wanted. It was also a chance for him to shove me away and call me a fag, a rumor he could then spread around.

"Come on, man. Whatchu got for me?"

What did I have for him? What did I want? I didn't know. All I had to go on were the facts of that bathroom and our past: the time I spotted a ten-dollar bill on the sidewalk outside the mall, and how Ted, always faster, beat me to it then refused to share one cent; all those days he'd push our teachers to the limits of their patience then find some way to turn their anger toward me, after which he'd pass a note saying something like *Best friends never nark. Your buddy 'til the end, Ted;* and of course our endless game of Gotcha Last where the last one to tag the other in the final seconds before our parting for the day had stuck that other, almost always me, with the burden of being IT until we met again.

"I'm going home," I said.

"Don't be a loser," Ted said. "You know I gotcha good."

He had. He'd done something that was both an invitation and a prank, and now he could laugh at me regardless of whether I got angry or tried to respond in kind. So I did the only thing there was to do besides standing there until I understood what any of it meant.

I left. I walked out of one future and into another where nothing was the same between Ted and me. I quit calling him, and those few times he called me to hang out there was a tension between us that wouldn't quite fade. We didn't play the same games. We lost interest in Gotcha Last or doing dead falls. We no longer wrestled. Instead of stealing army men it was cigarettes. Mostly we destroyed stuff. The one thing we didn't do was talk about what had happened in the bathroom.

The last time I hung out with Ted was near the end of that summer between seventh and eighth grade. We took a realistic-looking stuffed puppy from his little sister's bedroom, tied packaging twine around its neck, hid it behind a trash can near the curb then ran the twine into the bushes across the street where we waited. When the first car came by, a red Chevy Camaro driven by a young, blonde woman, Ted yanked that puppy out from behind the trashcan and into the street. She slammed on the brakes, skidding hard and driving over the thing before sideswiping a parked sedan. She got out crying and clacked over to the puppy in her skirt and high heels. I pulled on Ted's T-shirt. He jerked away and sat watching as she realized it was a stuffed animal, noticed the string, and began following it toward the bushes with her eyes.

"Come on," I hissed, "Let's go."

Ted stood straight up from our hiding place.

"Burned you, bitch!" he said.

By then I was on my feet and running. The scream of rage and frustration that came out of her was one of the ugliest sounds I've ever heard. Ted's laughter mixing in only made it worse.

That evening we took the alley to the back entrance of Hampton's Drugstore where we used to shoplift candy. We slouched along in the dusk, hands shoved deep into the pockets of our cutoffs as we kicked at cans and loose chunks of asphalt. A burning sliver of sun edged the tops of the stores lining the alley. Our long shadows stretched away from us.

Ted broke the silence. "You know that day I dared you in the bathroom?"

"What about it?"

"I was just fucking with you," he said.

Rage flared up inside me. I held it in. We kept on walking.

"It's okay," I said, "Forget it."

"You didn't tell anybody about what happened, did you?"

"No. I didn't tell anybody. I'm not going to tell anybody. What's to tell?"

"'Cause I was only fucking around. You know that, don't you?"

"I told you let's forget it."

"You promise you're not going to tell anybody."

I stopped suddenly and faced him.

"Didn't I just say I'm not going to fucking tell anybody?"

"Okay, okay. You don't have to get all pissed about it."

Ted pulled an unopened pack of Marlboro Reds out of his back pocket and began slapping the top down against the palm of his hand. "So you and me, we're cool, right?"

"Yeah. We're cool," I said.

Ted nodded and started working on the cellophane, peeling it from around the top of the pack before shaking the piece off his fingers into a gust of wind.

"Man, you shoulda seen Suzie Maselle at the park pool the other day," he said. "That bitch has some humongous tits."

"Don't call her that," I said.

"What?"

"Don't call her a bitch. She's not a bitch."

"I'm not saying she's a bitch. I'm saying she has some nice tits is all. I know you like her. I'm just fucking with you."

I stepped in closer. Eye to eye. "You sure like to fuck with me, don't you?"

We stood there, staring each other down in the twilight. Suddenly, I grabbed him by the shoulders and kissed him full on the mouth. I broke the kiss off as quickly as I'd started it, leaving him no time to respond. Then, one hand still on his shoulder, I punched him as hard as I could in the face.

Ted reeled back, staggered a step, but didn't fall or even drop his smokes. He gathered himself and eyed me narrowly as he put the back of his hand against his lip and glanced at the blood that came away.

He gave a quick snort. Shook his head. Tongued his teeth. "Shit, man, I think you maybe knocked one loose," he said.

I tensed, ready. I'd seen him fight, how he could flash out with his fists. He pulled a smoke from the pack and set it gingerly between his lips.

"Guess I had both of those coming," he said.

"Something like that," I said.

"Smoke?" he asked, offering me the pack.

"No," I said, "It's late. I need to get home."

"Sure you don't want one for the walk?" He was the one who seemed uncertain now, holding out a pack of stolen cigarettes to me in an alley at dusk.

"I'm sure," I said. "I gotta go."

As I turned away I heard the rasp of his lighter. His inhale followed sharply after, a sound like a breath taken in surprise. Then came the slow, exaggerated sigh of his exhaling.

"Later, lover," he said, and I hitched a step, but kept on walking.

The sliver of sun had dipped behind the buildings, the tops of which now looked to be on fire. Without turning around I raised my arm and flicked my hand in a way that said goodbye.

The next day at breakfast my mother told me Ted's family was moving; they'd bought a bigger house across town. I wondered why I hadn't seen a sign on their lawn or why Ted hadn't mentioned anything to me. I shrugged it off. When my mother asked why I didn't seem to care, I told her I did care, what did she want me to do, cry about it? She said to quit with the smart mouthing if I didn't want to get grounded. I shut up and went down into the basement to work on the 1-32$^{nd}$ scale Fokke-Wulf 190 I'd been meaning to finish for a while.

They moved sometime during those last weeks of summer while my family was on a vacation, driving from Detroit to San Francisco in a rented Winnebago. All through that trip, memories of Ted kept popping into my head. Not about the kiss or the punch, but the things I missed. In the darkness, we'd pass the blue eye of a TV glowing through a farmhouse window, and I'd find myself smiling, thinking about how Ted and me used to stay up late on Saturday night sleepovers, laughing our asses off at Count Ghoulio blowing up frogs with firecrackers during intermissions from movies like *Mars Needs Women*. I'd crouch to pull a bag of BBQ potato chips from the slot of a rest stop vending machine, and suddenly I was looking through a catcher's mask, trying to follow the wicked arc of Ted's curveball. Sometimes I'd just be zoning, staring off into the endless prairie, only to end up all the way back across

America where I'd conjure Ted's family pulling out of their driveway for the last time, Ted staring back at me from the rear window of their station wagon as they drove away.

That fall Ted started eighth grade at a junior high on the other side of town, and my mom gave me his new phone number, which I threw away. A family with two high school age daughters moved into Ted's old house. Sometimes on my way home after school I would see the girls talking with older boys, see them leaning into the open windows of the cars those boys had parked in the street. I never learned the girls' names. I never even got up the guts to wave hello as I walked by.

I grew nearly two inches that year, lost some baby fat, sprouted lean muscle and stopped thinking about Ted and what had happened in the bathroom and the alley. After dropping the weight, I discovered I was able to run surprisingly fast. I went out for track, won a few races, made some friends on the team, and started getting noticed by the girls at my school.

The next year Ted and I continued on to different high schools, different friends and completely separate lives. Ted eventually stepped into the role of troubled teen, stealing money and pills and booze from his parents, doing rehab more than once before finally getting dumped off some 4:00 a.m. like a torn bag of trash at the foot of his driveway, a bloody mess beaten nearly to death for selling bunk speed. I became obsessed with playing guitar and trying to start a rock band. I learned how to impress people by proving I could drink them under the table at parties, and I quickly mastered the dull art of getting wasted. But unlike Ted, who was doing it to act out, I was doing it to fit in.

I lost my virginity as a sophomore and had my share of girlfriends as high school went on. Yet, now and then during those years, the image of me kissing one of my buddies would pop suddenly into my head. A kind of echo of the first half of what had gone down in the alley that day. It never happened when you'd expect, but at the oddest times: as we were stepping into a liquor store to buy with our fake IDs; when we were driving around aimlessly, cranking AC/DC; when we were sitting in someone's basement smoking a joint; and as those surprising images faded, I'd remember Ted, wonder how he was, and a wave of something like regret would roll over me.

I know what I know about Ted's life beyond our friendship because my parents and Ted's parents are still good friends. I know that Ted, once clear of his troubles, turned out to be a good-looking, teetotaling, fashion-conscious man with dreams of modeling and an acting career. I know that on his way west he wandered from city to city and through a series of odd jobs before settling in as a waiter in San Francisco. I also know that beyond what my parents may have told his, he has no idea what has become of me—a divorced, childless, thirty-something copywriter working at a Detroit ad agency.

When I recently went to visit my parents in their new Florida condo, my mother mentioned she had been to Ted's wedding a month or so before. "I thought you might like to know," she said. She also said he was extremely charming and looked fantastic striking poses in his designer tuxedo. "He rivaled the bride," she told me, an odd description for a groom, I thought. Apparently he'd asked about me. "How's Danny?" He wanted to know. He mentioned he was sorry he couldn't invite me, the guest list was just too long, and he gave her his phone number. "I'd love to have a talk about the good old days," he said, "All that trouble we used to get into." I wondered if he thought much about the bathroom and the alley, *those* good old days. Was he just being polite or did he really expect me to call? Had he forgotten, or did he believe we would simply avoid talking about why our last moments together were so brutally intimate?

"What ever happened between you two?" my mother asked as she handed me the cocktail napkin with his name, number, and "*Call me!*" scribbled across it. I caught her studying my face as I looked up from the napkin and realized she'd waited until my father went out for his afternoon walk to tell me all of this. "I never understood why you two stopped being friends when it seemed like you were so close."

I stubbed out my cigarette in the ashtray and polished off my drink, setting the empty glass down on the onyx coaster as I sank back into the leather couch. The elastic tie had slipped away from the base of my ponytail. I reached up and cinched it tighter, ran my fingers through the long, scraggly goatee my mother hates, and searched for ways to explain that I had yet to forgive Ted for sitting there in front of the bathroom door and laughing at me, even after I told him to move. I had yet to forgive him for failing to let me go so I could decide on my own if I wanted to come back. But telling her those things meant explaining why. It meant describing how I shoved the door even harder, wedging Ted between it and the wall as I squeezed my way through. It meant showing him to her, naked on the bathroom floor, somehow hooking his hand around the edge of the door and scraping his fingernail along the tendon above my heel when I pushed past, my wincing at the sharp red line dragged down my skin as I heard him say, "Don't go. It's your turn." It meant admitting to her that when I kept going he knew my weakness well enough to use the words I'd have to carry with me if they didn't draw me back.

"Gotcha last."

"I guess we just lost touch," I said as I tapped another smoke out of the pack. "I mean, you know, once they moved and we went off to different schools. Then he started getting in trouble and everything."

It was all I could manage. Because once I started, I'd have to go on. Make us both another drink and tell her everything about Ted and me. Tell her how we began by yanking out the last of each other's baby teeth with pliers and doorknobs and twine. How we graduated from shoplifting candy and toys to stealing *Penthouse* and smoking cigarettes and burning things. I'd have to describe us doing our dead falls by the hospital parking lot as people with diseases drove slowly past looking for space. Those aren't things you want to share with your mother, long-buried memories and the questions they raise about you and your best friend getting too close before you knocked him back. I only knew one thing for certain: even after all those years I didn't have the words to explain how I felt about Ted. All I had was an image of two boys writhing and clutching at their chests, spinning out of control and falling down dead, even as they went on living.

## Blood Sacrifice

It's the burning that surprises him most, more so even than the brute shock of unexpected impact when the snowball, no, the *ice*-ball, drills magma into his ear. His hand darts to the side of his head. He staggers and turns to see the clot of them laughing and pointing from across the street. He does not know who they are, probably public school kids, all three of them a few years older, calling him *asshole*, *pussy*, *loser* to the wind ringing past his torn eardrum. He balls crisp air in his fists beneath the glazed trees. There's blood trickling from his ear, blood beginning to freeze against his neck when he steps into the street without checking for traffic. Walking right through the sliding trombone horn of a passing car, a righteous rage fills him, this Catholic boy who'd been minding his own business on the way home from Catholic school on his thirteenth birthday.

They're still laughing when his boot touches the opposite curb.

"Which one of you threw it?" he says, "Which one?"

"I threw it, church boy. What are you gonna do, forgive me?"

Later, he'll wonder if God saw him, like a hockey player, fling his gloves down. Later, he'll wonder if God heard the lip split, colored the blood blooming across bright teeth, felt the furious anger of the two boys tangling down to the frozen sidewalk. Later, he'll recall that it seemed like Jesus was inside his fists, guiding them to land the shame of each wallop to eye, nose, and the other cheek turned because right now nothing touches him except the hands that finally pull him off, drag him back, hold him down so bloody anger can finally stand, wipe its bleeding mouth on the back of its jacket sleeve and spit, "Motherfucker, it's your turn now."

And so the world sits upon his chest, pins him to the ground, raining blows until he cannot feel, struggling on his back, squinting up at the whiteout sky. No safety boys. No parents. No saviors waving pink slips. It ends only when they grow weary of beating him, kicking him once more in the gut before leaving him there to slowly lever himself back up into the muted afternoon.

Last spring he picked a bouquet of flowers for his mother from the flowerbeds that line this street, and she thought this sweet even though she told him it was forbidden to pick things from others' gardens. Now he walks home past the barren beds, already feeling her trembling hands gingerly pressing a cold cloth against his torn and swollen face as she tries not to let him see her cry.

The fight and the thought of his mother's pain have him turned inside out, make him feel like a jacket stomped into the ice with the sleeves pulled through and flung wide. He tests his tongue against a loose tooth, touches his nose and winces, hoping it's not broken too bad. Behind him, leading all the way back to the circle of the fight, are sprays of red and pink where he's spat in the snow. Ahead, the cold day remains perfectly vacant. No cars pass. The neatly shoveled sidewalks are empty.

He stops and looks off into the void sky. For years he's been told to expect nothing; God demands faith without proof, without question. He listens for any message beyond the thudding pulse of his torn ear, only to hear a jagged echo of the times he's wept over his failure to live up to the example of gentle, brave, perfect Jesus. He thinks of that perfect Jesus, who was answered with silence after asking, "Why have you forsaken me?" as he suffered on the cross. Jesus, who could accept such silence even as he surrendered his spirit.

## No Prints, No Negatives

The first time I heard my dad say *fuck* we were driving through Utah in a rented Winnebago. I was thirteen, and my dad believed I was ready to learn what it meant to be an American. He believed I was ready to see for myself the realities of the homeland I'd soaked up through the TV and read about in history class. So at the end of summer he rented a Winnebago and drove my mom and me west from the suburbs of Detroit toward San Francisco, out into the sideways glances of the archetypal cross-country family road-trip. Out into the landscape of the American Dream.

During those years, my dad was often gone, traveling around the country and the world on business trips as an auto executive. Our nice home on Lakeland Drive said it all: he was a damn good auto industry PR man. He knew celebrities and spoke at auto shows. He had a six-figure salary. He was responsible for the public image of a corporation worth billions of dollars. Etcetera. Though I didn't get to see him as much as I would have liked, he was what some would call an ideal father. Like many fathers, he'd shown his son a few things about walking it off and throwing spirals, but he also had enough pull to get me down into the pit at Daytona and introduce me to Richard Petty and Dale Earnhardt. Maybe he wasn't there to tuck me in every night or watch me dive into that first crash landing the day I took the training wheels off my bike, but he got me a seat in 15th row between the checkered flag and the fourth turn, and when Petty nailed the wall, sending a tire spinning into the stands, he worried his way down from the press box to make sure I was okay.

As far as I knew back then, my dad had grown up happy in a large, lower middle class Irish Catholic family, the youngest son of nine children born to an immigrant newspaper printer and his wife. His was a 1930s childhood of ice trucks and actual milkmen, sandlot baseball teams, and an old Jewish guy bumping a junky truck down the alley behind his house to a thickly accented mantra of "Pots mended. Knives sharpened. You want, I got."

In the family photo album there was a black and white picture of my dad in knickers, another of him at his fourth birthday party in a cowboy outfit sitting on the back of that ubiquitous shaggy, spotted pony. One day, while flipping through the album, I noticed the dark edge of a negative hidden behind his navy portrait and slid it out and held it up to the light. I went and found a magnifying glass.

If you were to print the picture you'd see my dad sitting inside a nightclub somewhere dressed in his navy blues. He's rail thin and smiling thickly. It looks like he might even still have some acne. His eyes are heavy-lidded, and his face shiny with sweat. He's probably not even twenty, but there he is, in reverse, leaning toward the small, round, bottle-littered table along with two of his Navy buddies, all of them frozen in the middle of having a sloppy good time.

"That was Hawaii near the end of WWII, years before I met your mother," he said when I brought the album to him. "A bunch of jarheads came in right after that, started calling us mate-a-lots and deck monkeys. We ended up breaking the place apart and getting tossed out." He tucked the negative back behind the serious-faced navy portrait. "Same night I got this," he said, pointing to a scar I'd never noticed before, a short, faded slice above his left eyebrow. "Courtesy of Budweiser."

Now nearly fifty in the mid 1970s, he was the archetypal self-made man ready to serve up America to a son born late in his life, the naïve little kid in the windowed sleeper above the Winnebago's cab whose biggest problems were worrying about when his walkman batteries were going to die and finding back issues of *CONAN* and *Sgt. Fury and the Howling Commandos*.

It was August when we left. We rolled past Chicago, bridged the Mississippi and shot across the Great Plains, driving through Davenport, Des Moines, and Sioux City before climbing into the Black Hills and the Badlands to find the presidents blasted onto the face of Mount Rushmore. Along the way, it all seemed true: majestic purple mountains anchored the horizon beyond endless, amber seas of grain waving in the wind beneath spacious skies. But there were also sun-blasted reservation trailers orbited by chained dogs carving dry moats into baked dirt yards, and the remnants of dead towns where the skeletons of stripped cars and abandoned buildings clung to the dry stem of the road like shriveled fruit. It seemed my dad wanted me to notice this kind of thing as well. "It's a damn shame the way those people live," he'd said as we passed a drunken Indian staggering along the shoulder of a two-lane highway that marked the border of a reservation. What didn't occur to me at the time was to ask him who he thought was to blame.

We continued west toward San Francisco. I leaned my chest against the iron railing and peered down into the vast pit of the Grand Canyon. I stood in a knot of tourists and watched Old Faithful go off like clockwork in Yellowstone. I stared out the windows at rose-tinted rock formations filling with deep pools of shadow in the late afternoon sun as we descended into Salt Lake City and stopped at a light in the middle of downtown.

My dad had just finished explaining the religious subtleties of the Mormons to me. "Do they really get to have more than one wife? How come they wear an undershirt all the time?" These were the stupid questions I'd asked in those last uncomplicated minutes before three guys in a black, souped-up Mustang convertible pulled next to us at the light and revved it loud enough to get my mom's attention.

"What the fuck are you looking at, bitch?" the driver shouted over the engine. His two buddies laughed. They had long, greasy hair. Badly drawn tattoos pocked their forearms. One of them was actually chewing on a toothpick. My mom looked away.

"Yeah, that's right. Nobody fucking eyeballs me. Ya cooze."

My dad leaned across the wide space between the front captain's chairs, toward the passenger window. The muscles corded out on his arm as he pointed a stiff finger at the Mustang driver. Just as he opened his mouth to say something, the light changed and the person in the car behind us pressed hard on their horn, startling him.

"Fuck you, old man," the Mustang driver said, flipping us the finger as he stomped on the accelerator. The Mustang peeled out, snapped a quick fishtail and shot away into traffic, disappearing in a blue haze of burnt rubber. White-knuckling the wheel, my dad clenched his jaw and gassed it a bit too hard. The Winnebago lurched into motion as my mom threw him a nervous glance. Of course we could never catch them, but I could see he was thinking about trying.

"What the hell was that all about, Teresa?" he asked. "What'd you say to those guys?"

"I didn't say anything. I just looked at him and he started swearing at me."

"Are you sure you didn't say something?"

"Francis! Of course I'm sure."

"What do you mean you looked at him? What kind of look did you give him?"

"I didn't give him any kind of look. I just looked at him."

"Well quit looking at people."

We passed through the rest of Salt Lake City in silence, then found ourselves back in the desert, heading south toward the neon oasis of Las Vegas. I no longer had the stomach for scenery. I was too tangled with trying to figure out why someone would be so rude and ugly to my mom for no apparent reason. Never in my life had I heard anyone talk to her that way. I tried to go back to Conan killing monsters and Sgt. Fury kicking Nazi ass, but I just couldn't concentrate. I kept wishing I were older, stronger. I fantasized about beating the crap out of those guys, throwing them down one at a time at my mother's feet and standing over each of them as they begged her forgiveness. There was an ugly tension in the Winnebago now. We all seemed angry at intangibles, and we weren't talking about why.

After some time, I got up from the dinette and went to my mom. I stood there next to her chair as the soft, warm pastels of the sunset-splashed desert sky came at us through the Winnebago's gigantic windshield.

"Are you okay, mom?" I put my hand on her shoulder. "Those guys were jerks. They shouldn't have talked to you like that. Nobody should talk to you like that."

"Dan, you're not supposed to be walking around while we're moving," my dad said. "Sit down and put your seatbelt on."

It was the first I'd heard of that. For the last two weeks I'd been walking all over the place while we were driving, climbing up and down from the sleeper, sitting at the dinette table reading comics, going to the bathroom, getting iced teas out of the fridge for my dad.

"But you never said…"

"I said sit down and look at the scenery. There's lots of beautiful country around here. What am I doing all this driving for if you're not going to pay attention to what's going on out there?"

My mom put her hand over mine. "Do as your father says, honey. I'm fine. Some people are just rude, that's all. I feel sorry for them."

I sat down at the dinette table strewn with my comics, my walkman and my cassettes and felt around between the cushions for the straps of the lap belt. Utah scrolled past, darkening. I wondered how a place that had looked so spectacular to me only a few hours before could suddenly seem so alien and desolate.

Somewhere after the town of Spanish Fork the flow of traffic slowed to a crawl as all of the southbound lanes were directed to the shoulder. An endless line of cars stretched away from us to the horizon. My dad started grumbling and kept asking me to refill his glass of iced tea from the plastic gallon jug in the fridge. He no longer seemed bothered by the fact that I had to get up and walk around to do it.

The jug was half empty by the time we reached the cause of the jam: one car pushed up tightly against the rear end of another, a third skidded sideways a little farther down the road. All in all it wasn't much. No spider-webbed windshields. No crushed trunks. No accordioned front ends. It didn't look like something that should take so long to get around or move, but there was still no tow-truck in sight. By the time we pulled even with the single, annoyed cop directing traffic around the wreck my dad was frustrated enough to say something.

"This is ridiculous," he told the cop. "What's taking so long to clear the road?"

"People like you slowing down to ask me stupid questions," the cop said. "Keep it moving."

Hours later, a pot-hole jolted me awake into the darkness of the sleeper. On my stomach, looking out the narrow front window, I watched our headlights ticking off slashes of white line to the rustle of comic book pages and wondered where we were. I had no idea what time it was, but the road was empty, and the breeze felt late. My parents were talking beneath me, their voices tight and muffled with hostile restraint.

"Francis, when are we going to stop?" my mom asked. "I need sleep."

"Just go in the back and lie down," he said. "It's a motor home, for Christ's sake."

"You know I can't sleep while we're moving. It makes me sick."

"We need to make up time. We're way behind."

"Way behind what? It's not like we have a schedule. You're just all jacked up on caffeine."

"Go lie down, Teresa."

"FINE," she said. Metal clacked as she unbuckled her seatbelt and flung it aside. A few seconds later I heard her rip open the curtain to the bedroom in the back then rake it closed behind her.

"Oh, cut it with the drama!" my dad barked. "I'm just trying to get us down the road."

Silence.

"Okay, fine already, I'll stop. Jesus. Just let me find a decent place to pull over."

"Bunch of goddamn bullshit," he mumbled.

Lying there above his head, I tried to keep perfectly still and pretend this wasn't happening. It seemed as if my moving or breathing too hard would only make matters worse and

somehow cause all of our lives to come totally unraveled.
I'd never heard my parents talk to each other this way before.
Sure, they fought. They must have fought, they were married,
but up until then they'd managed to never really do it in front
of me. I stared out the front window of the sleeper. The
Winnebago's headlights soaked the road, causing the mile
markers and exit signs to pop up suddenly from the darkness
like the badly drawn one-dimensional villains and monsters
that spring out at each cart during cheap carnival haunted
house rides.

Finally, after my dad's promise to stop in just a few more
miles had come to mean three more towns and a sign showing
only fifteen miles to the California border, my mother called
her woozy anguish from the bed in the back.

"Francis!"

Silence. Warm desert wind through the open windows. The
Winnebago's wheels thumping lightly over flaws in the road.

"Francis!"

Silence.

"Francis! Can we please stop driving?!"

"FUCK! Jesus! Alright, fine!" he shouted. "Just quit bitching!"

The motor home rattled and shook as my dad pulled to the
side of the empty two-lane road and slammed it into Park. I
could feel his weight shifting around in the front seat as he
threw off his seatbelt and sat there swearing at my mom under
his breath. I shoved my face into my pillow. I couldn't
understand why he didn't just pull off the road miles ago like
she'd asked. She really did have motion sickness; she got sick
on airplanes and when they went on cruises. He knew that.
Obviously something tremendous and irrevocable had gone
wrong with all our lives. It was as if that Mustang driver's
words had somehow infected us and made my mom and dad
hate each other. Why else would they talk to each other that

way? It was obvious to me: we would turn around tomorrow and drive back home so they could get divorced.

My dad stood up. His heavy steps shook the motor home as he stamped toward the bed in the back where my mom lay in silence. Again the curtain hissed open and closed, and I was afraid for what would happen between them next, though I had no idea what that might be.

For some time there was only the engine ticking and the creaks of the Winnebago settling. Then came the low words as my parents started talking, and finally, my mother sharply saying, "No." My dad pushed angrily through the curtain. He opened the side door, closed it firmly then keyed it locked behind him. His feet crunched into the shoulder gravel. Through the sleeper's front window I watched his silhouette disappearing into the night as he headed up the road toward a bar with a red neon sign flashing *Spanky's*. I fell asleep trying to convince myself that he had to come back for us eventually.

I have no idea how many motorcycles roared past before I woke up, but after one, then another, and another, and another, and another shook the Winnebago, I finally rolled over and looked out the sleeper window. The parking lot of Spanky's was filled with motorcycles glinting in the glow of a low and gigantic desert moon. Motorcycles leaned beneath the building's floodlights in a long, gleaming line stretching away from the front door. Outlaws, violent, greasy looking men in heavy boots, torn jeans and black leather jackets stalked around drinking beer, laughing, yelling, shoving each other, slapping at the asses of the women who kept walking in and out of the bar with armloads of bottles. They were popping wheelies, racing all over the place, clouds rising in whorls as they cut tight circles in the dust. It was the most amazing and terrifying thing I'd ever seen.

At the far end of the line of motorcycles, a knot of people gathered around something. They were shouting, cheering someone on, pressing inward. It was hard to tell from a distance, but it looked like a fight, an accelerated version of the schoolyard situations I knew too well: two people struggling on the ground, or maybe one person on top of another, lunging at them again and again. I caught what looked like a flash of my dad's red shirt in the motorcycle headlights, and a sick feeling kicked loose in my chest, climbing up into my throat as I groped around in the dark for the binoculars he'd given me at the beginning of the trip so I could get a close-up view of the real America. My dad was being beaten to death by a bunch of bikers out in front of a biker bar a few miles from the California border, and all I could think was, "What has he done now?" Had he snapped at one of them the way he snapped at my mom because he was still pissed off about not being able to come to her defense in Salt Lake City? Had he told one of those bikers to fuck off when they'd gotten in his face for being in their bar? Would they come after us once they finished with him? Was all of this something we had coming because of what we did or didn't do in between the Mustang driver's hateful words and now? Only one thing seemed clear: the man who'd locked the Winnebago's side door and stormed off into the night was not the tall, calm dad who almost always came home from his office whistling. He was someone who needed saving.

I had to wake up my mom. In a flash I saw her smashing the Winnebago into the crowd of them. Saw myself jumping out the side door with the fire extinguisher and spraying it in their faces as I grabbed my bloody dad and helped him back in. I imagined us peeling out of there, hundreds of bikers hot on our tail as we tried to get in touch with the cops on the CB radio. I could see my dad thanking me, telling me he was proud of his son. There I was, bringing him a towel to help stop the blood. There I was, throwing things out the Winnebago's windows in hopes of seeing those bikers wad themselves into a tangled wreck in our wake. He would apologize to my mom, say he was sorry for yelling and swearing and tell her that he loved her. "I know," she'd grin and stomp that gas pedal down. I started shaking. They were killing him. I turned away from the window to call out.

"What is going on out there?" my mother said from the back.

"We have to save him!" I was about to tear aside the sleeper curtains, leap down and shout it.

"It's just some guys on motorcycles, Teresa," came my dad's annoyed, tired voice.

I edged one of the curtains aside and looked through the gap. He was sitting at the dinette table in the dark, part of a six-pack near his elbow, a can in his hand.

"Just some guys on motorcycles? Francis, look out the window."

"I have been."

"Well, what are you going to do about it?"

"What's there to do? It's a free country."

My mom hurried up from the back. She stood over him at the table in her nightgown, "There is no way in hell we're staying here," she said.

My dad drained his beer and set it down. He stared out the window at the bikers, considering, then gave a heavy exhale as if trying to let something go. He pushed himself up from the table, hooked his fingers through the empty loops of the six-pack and carried the remaining cans with him toward the captain's chair, my mom following behind him, whispering something at the back of his head. I couldn't quite make out what they were saying over the revving motorcycle engines and shouts as they strapped themselves in. Sharp things, hushed and short. I think they wanted to believe that somehow I was sleeping through it all. My dad turned the engine over, dropped it into Drive, and pulled us from the shoulder back onto the road.

The sweaty, prickling shock of adrenaline still ran through me as I tamped down my tears of relief. Nearing the bar, it became clear the knot of shouting people was circled around a man and a woman writhing on the ground. She was on top of him, bobbing up and down, naked in the warm night except for a red bandanna wrapped around her head, her long bleach-blonde hair spilling out the back of it. There was a look of wild joy, almost rage, on her face.

"Oh, my God," my mom gasped. "We have to call the police."

"Looked like she was enjoying herself to me."

"What! What did you say?"

"I said it's none of our business."

"Francis!"

"Okay. Okay. Fine. I'll see if I can raise somebody on the CB."

As we passed the crowd, I locked eyes with a shirtless man at the outer edge of the circle. He had an eagle tattooed swooping across his chest. He raised his beer bottle when we roared by, thrust out his waggling tongue from a mouth missing more than a few teeth. What a joke I was to him, some dumb little kid in a camper, shock stitched across my tear-streaked face, my hands pressed up against glass.

My mom and dad were short with each other the next morning and throughout the next day as we walked through the gaudy chaos of Caesar's Palace. This quick stop at the casino wasn't about my dad getting in a few hands of blackjack or my mom using the numbers of my birthday to play roulette. Neither of my parents were gamblers. This was meant to be a lesson for me, my dad's unspoken comment on a world of unnecessary risk inhabited by bleary-eyed men who ran their hands through their hair as they stared at the empty space where their stacks of chips had once been. This was meant to be a warning about the misplaced priorities that I should read in the utterly blank faces of women who slung drooling, doped babies over their shoulders as they fed ravenous, unforgiving slot machines toward dawn.

Halfway through the casino, I was sucked into the gravitational pull of a gigantic, flashing slot machine that seemed to be the center of it all: BIG TRIPLE DIAMOND DELUXE. It was on a pedestal all its own; crimson and gold and taller than my dad and wider than the both of us standing there next to each other.

"You want to try your luck on this thing?" he asked.

I nodded. The blank look on his face made it impossible to tell if my answer had disappointed him.

"How much money do you have on you?"

"I don't have any money," I said.

"Well, how can you gamble if you don't have any money?

I shrugged.

"Tell you what, I'll loan you the dollar. But if you lose you owe me."

My father went to the cashier's cage and came back with a silver dollar.

"Good luck," he said, handing it to me.

I hefted the coin in my palm. It was the bicentennial job, the one with Eisenhower on the head and a cracked liberty bell and a meteor-riddled moon on the flipside. The moon reminded me of the night before and the bikers. I wondered what they thought about the idea of risk and luck and decided they probably believed that risk came with the territory and the only kind of luck was the kind you make for yourself. I put the coin into the slot and heard it rattle down through the machine's metal guts. The slot's arm was as thick around as my own, and my hand barely covered the black ball at its end. My dad and I stood together watching the machine's three wheels spin until their staggered stop. Two silver dollars clunked down into the stainless steel tray. I reached in.

"Ha," my dad snorted in disbelief. "Looks like you got lucky, kid. That almost never happens. Just remember, in the end they've rigged this place for you to lose."

"Here's your dollar," I said, offering my dad one of the coins. It felt good to win, but I also felt a little guilty, the same the way I would years later after the first time I beat him at racquetball.

"No, you keep them both. We'll call it even."

"Excuse me, sir." A man in a dark suit strode up to my father out of nowhere. "I'm sure you're aware that children are not allowed to gamble in this or any other casino."

My father bristled. "He's not gambling. You think I'd let my son gamble? We were just passing through. I let him put a dollar in the slot for me. I was trying to teach him a lesson."

The man in the suit glanced down at the two silver dollars in my palm. I shoved them into my pocket.

"I'm sorry, sir, but I'm going to have to ask you to leave."

My dad sized the man up, his eyes lingering on the walkie-talkie microphone attached to his lapel. "So you're kicking us out?"

"I'm asking you politely to leave, sir. Now, please."

The man was firm, but he was treating us with respect. I saw something shift in my dad's face. He understood this man was only doing his job. "Okay. I get you," my dad said, "Sorry about this. I didn't know."

"Of course, sir. It's not a problem, sir."

My dad put his arm around my shoulder, which wasn't something he usually did. "Let's go find your mom. I think you've seen enough of this place."

We caught up with my mom in a jewelry store in the Forum Shops. She was admiring a pair of sapphire earrings in a glass case.

"You like those?" my dad asked.

"They're beautiful, but they're too much."

He leaned over the case and looked at the price. "They're not too much. Besides, Christmas is only five months away." He smiled at her.

She reached out and took his hand, "Oh, Francis, no, you don't have to, really. It's okay."

"I know," he said. "I want to."

She kissed him on the cheek. "If you insist," she said and walked off smiling to find a sales lady to open the display case. After she'd gone, my dad gave me a nudge. "That's the kind of thing you can do for someone you love when you don't waste your money and time gambling," he said.

That night, I heard quiet laughter coming from the bedroom in the back of the Winnebago. The next morning it was as if my parents had never even driven through Salt Lake City, or fought in front of me, or made an escape during the night of the motorcycles. It was as if, for them, nothing bad had even happened.

For my part, I couldn't shake those dark outlaws laughing and stumbling through the dust-swirled high beams of Spanky's gravel parking lot. That naked woman with her head thrown back in ecstasy. That guy with the eagle rising off his chest. They were all I thought about—people living lives I could not understand no matter how I tried. Their America came at them in a blast of hot wind as they thundered in a pack down rolling stretches of highway. They did what they wanted, not what they were told, and they would probably rather die than live a life like the one I knew then, like the one I suspected my parents hoped I would eventually give my own children.

The day before we were supposed to drop off the Winnebago and fly back to Detroit, it was broken into on the edge of Chinatown in San Francisco, and my mom's new earrings and my dad's camera bag containing all the film he'd shot during our vacation were stolen.

"God damn it!" he shouted when we came back loaded down with cheap Chinatown trinkets to find the front passenger door of the Winnebago sprung open, "They took everything, even the negatives."

"I think they stole my new earrings!" my mom said as she searched around the big console in front of the dashboard where she'd left them.

Maybe my memory was still stained with what had happened the week before, but the anger seemed to rise in my dad too quickly, as if he had still not fully returned to himself, and I started worrying that he never would. Then I understood: it wasn't him who'd changed. We all have two faces, one of them unknown to those who love us. We've all slid a negative of ourselves beneath the picture we show to others.

My dad had gotten some of the film developed at a twenty-four hour place in Las Vegas. I'd seen the prints and the negatives tucked behind them. I knew what had been taken. There would be no photo album with pictures of the grinning innocent pointing up the nose of Lincoln at Mt. Rushmore. No pictures of me looking down into the Grand Canyon. No pictures of me standing in the middle of the Bonneville Salt Flats with arms outstretched. No pictures of my mom and dad standing in front of a sign for the Mystery Spot. Every single photograph from our trip was gone. All the evidence of before and after the night of the motorcycles captured on my face, in my folded arms, in the way I'm leaning like a punk against some Chinatown lamppost with my hands shoved deep into my pockets and a wise-ass grin cracked just wide enough for the future of a dangled cigarette. No proof that anything had changed. No prints. No negatives.

But they're out there somewhere. I can feel them traveling down the byways of junk and discarded things that pulse just below the surface of this nation. They're part of the underbelly, mixed in with the refuse of those people and places most of us just avoid or pretend not to see. My mom and dad and every other upstanding American like them would have you believe those memories are long buried, decomposing in a California landfill. I like to think they were found by some naïve kid who's put them in a photo album he can't set down. A kid like me who's been pulled into that space between the prints and the negatives. A kid like me who saw the picture then saw through.

## Black Sheep Missive

Back in high school, when I'm fucking up much less seriously, I have my friends over for drinks on Saturday nights when my parents are out. Having graduated from watering my old man's whiskey, I use my doctored ID to get away from the Liquor Mart with a bottle and a few cases of cheap beer. My friends, guys with nicknames like Dogger, Rockhead, Joey Bagga, Hula, Carp, The Bane, and B-All-Right, dudes who call me DOA, have their own sources, and they bring what they can when they can.

Wherever whatever comes from, the party always ends up in a tape loop of The Rolling Judas Zeppelin cranked to TEN as I take run of my parent's large, lakefront home. I paw the current girlfriend on the living room couch while my wasted buddies argue at poker, grope their own girls, suck down beer bongs at the kitchen sink, try not to puke in the odd corner on their stumble to the bathroom.

Around midnight I kick everybody to the curb, straighten out the knocked over knick-knacks, bag the poker chips, and crash. Only to awaken late on bright Sunday, twisted straight into the long hangover of a condom wrapper or some stub of roach or the bottle cap that found its place between the cushions or in some crack—the one and only thing I'd missed, the landmine that turns Mom into an explosion as she unearths it from behind a potted plant.

Oh, the black, time-warped magic in the way those luminous, throbbing awakenings suddenly dissolve through the years into this present tense where I am failing to find myself forever loaded, cool, righteous, young, and eternally immune to the possibilities of pot-belly premature bald razor burn now that I'm too far gone for my old man to shoulder his frame into the doorway of this shitty, low rent apartment, holding up whatever it is my mom has handed off to him, the knot of his all-day tie torn loose as if to say: God damn it, boy, this is no way to make a future.

## Visitation

He takes the highway east toward a family reunion of sorts, the setting sun blazing low and red at his back, causing him to squint and look away each time he tries to check his rearview mirror. It's been a few years since he's seen the oldest of his three sisters, the one who married and moved across the country while he was still in the second grade. The same one who just now got divorced.

He rolls along, pulled by the cruise control, rehashing his childhood, sifting his memory for something to help explain what this sister is supposed to mean to him. Nothing comes to mind, no moment or word they shared while she was still his big sister living at home and not a housewife in Texas with three children of her own. It's as if that part of their lives from before she moved away had never been. And he's forced to consider, yet again, how he's struck a wedge between himself and all the rest of them, his entire family: the parents he hasn't seen for over a month, the other two sisters, still married, who he also hardly ever sees and rarely calls. There's no reason he can find to justify his need for this distance, but he's forced to admit it's something he's never done much to change.

He settles finally on a memory from the summer after his freshman year in high school: the oldest sister has returned from Texas with the debut grandchild. It's a hot August night; his sister is twenty-something, golden-haired in the dim light of her childhood bedroom. Smiling, she holds out his infant niece. He takes her, the first of all his sisters' children, mothers her to his chest, and she pukes on him, baby puke, thin and milky. His sister laughs with embarrassment and takes the baby back. That baby is eighteen now, an attractive, almond-eyed young woman he doesn't really know smiling out at him from the picture he's stuck to his refrigerator door. Between the three of his sisters, five more nieces and nephews he barely knows have followed her.

Such ruminations have left him considering the vacuum of years that fills the space between an infant's uneasy stomach and her high school diploma; the arc of a young marriage's ruin traced to a middle-aged sister's returning home for the first time since her ugly, complicated divorce; the self-imposed exile fueling the longings of a son who usually keeps his longings to himself. The meaning of these things is bigger than his family in particular, he knows, and as the city rises before him and the traffic presses in he decides that if one thing unites all our shades of loneliness it's the many ways we settle for the absences we choose.

They lean over pasta in the suburban dining room of the second sister, the one he sees slightly more than the others because, like him, she stayed in the state where they grew up. The kids, his nieces and nephews, all teenagers now, eat at a separate table nearby. Staring across the span of his family, stunned by the realization of how little he truly knows any of them or what their secret hearts desire, he feels as if he's been summoned to retrieve them from the separate places to which they've been assigned.

He sits across from his parents, next to the oldest sister. "Three years," she says. "Has it really been that long? When are you going to come visit us in Houston?" She means this invitation, of course, but he has trouble imagining what such a visit would be like, what they would have to say to each other, what they would do. She left to become someone else before he was old enough to really know her, and he became who he is without her around. Now they are people with jobs, responsibilities, and, it seems, little more than blood and distance in common.

Since her divorce she's taken to running marathons. Recently, he looked for her on TV when she ran in New York City. He quickly realized it had been so long since he'd seen her he probably wouldn't be able to pick her out of the crowd. By the time he'd stopped watching, he'd found a number of women who might have been her. Now that he's with her, he doubts any of them were. He notices the worry lines worked into her face and realizes he's never in his life seen her run a single step. Still, he feels an urge to tell her the one true thing he knows about her: she has changed since he's seen her last, been awakened in ways she was not before her divorce. Everything he imagines she's been through—her husband's infidelity, his squeezing her in court over every single penny going to support his own children, her days and nights alone, her returning to work after years as a homemaker, being middle-aged and stepping nervously, reluctantly back into the world of dating and men—all of it has made her stronger, and somehow more beautiful. It is, despite the pain and ugliness, a good thing that has happened to her. He doesn't know what she'd think of his version of her truth, so he offers a toast instead, "To being here," he says and puts the cup against his lips.

After dinner the kids scatter and he stands in the doorway of the kitchen watching his sisters take to the dishes with an automatic efficiency they must have learned in that past he does not recall. Earlier, when they were done with eating, but still sitting at the table ritually recounting the family history, his mother told them about the birth of the third sister: "I saw rats crawling all over the ceiling when I had her. They gave me morphine after the delivery. I remember it was raining, and there were Venetian blinds in the room that were swaying from the breeze coming through the open window, and the shadows of the raindrops were shooting up the wall and changing into rats, thousands of rats all over the bed and the ceiling. In the hall I thought I heard someone talking who I swear to this day was saying my baby was missing a leg and an arm. 'Bring me my baby, bring me my baby,' I kept screaming. But they wouldn't listen."

Things gone wrong and missing. Chances lost. This is what he is thinking about when their mother comes into the kitchen and says to him jokingly, "You know, with the Caesarian scar you gave me and now the hysterectomy I could probably play connect the dots on my stomach." She toys absently with the edge of her un-tucked blouse as if she is about to lift it and show off the scars.

"Looks like no more bikinis for you, mom," the second sister winks. The first sister, the oldest, his stranger, says nothing. She turns her head away to stare out at the darkness collecting in the window above the sink. But for once he refuses to look away; he wants his mother to raise her shirt and show them all her stomach so he can trace those scars he has never seen. He's ready to wake his napping father off the couch, blacken the TV eye that's glued his nieces and nephews to the carpet, call the third, absent, sister on the phone so she can listen in as he holds the receiver to his mother's scar-dimpled belly. He sees himself circling the whole of this family around to tell them that the missing parts of their many lives, the parts he's missed, ring through his mind, and he is tired of only imagining who they are and how they must live. He finally understands: nothing will change until someone speaks to the spaces that have settled in between them; until someone reaches out to draw their eyes along the map of scars that connects them all.

## How to Time an Engine

Know the guts of that tin can like no one else. Go shirtless, skin sheened with oil and diesel. Duck past the coffee pot swinging from a lanyard as the pounding engines shake. Fire the pistons that turn the screws. Churn out the speed destroyers die and live by. Wring more knots out of the *Edwards*. Prowl the Solomon Islands on a mission to derail the Tokyo Express. Knife your ship through The Slot above the ruptured hulls of Ironbottom Sound. Barely outrun the Divine Winds and grin a tight line at the telling shock of a wing sheared off by the fantail, a Kamikaze's fuselage slamming into your destroyer's drowning wake. Be a salvo in the hunter-killer convoys, a warrant machinist, and no one's father yet.

Get honorably discharged from that life. Return home to Detroit in 1945. Raise six kids after burying a wife who died too young in a car crash. In your eighties, point a sailboat into the setting sun while holding fast to a can of beer.

Never say much about the World War in your past. Keep it all below decks. Tell no one about seeing flak blossom into those questions luck asks of aim. Leave it to others to speak of the torpedo bomber, a type the Japanese called "Heavenly Mountain," and your shipmates called a "Jill," peeling off from her sisters "Kate" and "Betty" and keening down through the explosive sky. Leave it to others to wonder at all the synchronicities housed inside a torpedo glanced off the water. A torpedo bouncing across the waves toward a speeding destroyer with perfectly timed engines pushed near to bursting by your hand. Pull the back of that hand across your grimy brow in the roaring engine room directly beneath the ship's twin stacks. Know those twin stacks are exactly far enough apart for a torpedo to leap over the gunwale and spin harmlessly in between. In between the story of your nearly taken life and all that will happen to you after.

# Moon with Princess

Last time I was in Florida visiting my old man, he went on the nod during the baseball game we were watching on TV. Looking at him, grey-haired, gravity wracked and lightly snoring in his recliner, it dawned on me: I'd been calling him my old man, though not to his face, ever since I was a teenager, that is, for nearly twenty years. Pushing eighty, he still had his health and his wits, for the most part, but the clock was clearly winding down. He was getting increasingly forgetful, he'd lost interest in golf, and he and my mother liked to talk about "the final solution" over those late dinners we shared when I came down. Even though this only meant moving from their expensive condo to an exclusive facility intended to gradually usher them into fully assisted living, it was difficult not to think about the fact that my old man had now absolutely become what I'd been calling him for so many years.

Touching the knickknacks he'd collected on his travels and the awards and mementos he'd been given by business associates always made me feel close to him in a way I didn't feel when we did things like sit around in silence watching baseball on TV. With my mom out shopping, I saw my chance. I went off to wander the condo and search for my old man in the artifacts of his past. I touched the bayonet given to him by the AMVets for his help in the fight against muscular dystrophy, the mounted hubcap you could raise to reveal a flask underneath from the Detroit Press Club, a mess tray from the USS Arizona, each little compartment of which was filled with a snapshot from his visit. I considered these and other things that marked moments in his life I knew little, if anything, about. Eventually, I found myself standing in his bedroom closet holding a hatbox I'd pulled from the top shelf. Inside were his World War II Navy Pacific Theater medals and a black and white photograph of him interviewing a midget princess back when he was a reporter for *The Detroit Times*.

My old man is six-foot-two, and the princess looks to be maybe two-and-a-half feet tall, so it was a good photo opportunity: a snapshot of the thirty-something, jet-haired reporter in an angled fedora and tan trench coat, pencil pressed against the notepad on his thigh as he crouches down across from that tiny woman in her miniature evening gown with a little mink stole wrapped around her shoulders and a child-sized diamond tiara in her hair. I should also mention she was old, quite grandmotherly, and a perfectly symmetrical midget, not a dwarf. If she'd been photographed without my old man around for scale, you'd have trouble telling her from any wealthy, little old lady.

I'd heard bits here and there, mostly through my mother, about the life my old man lived before I was born, this mythic life where he'd go out into the night to get let under the tape at a murder scene or watch the cops sift through millions in counterfeit bills, but this old photograph was the first evidence I'd ever seen. The image only reaffirmed the legends my childhood mind had created around his absence. There they were, forever frozen against the darkness, that toddler-sized old lady staring up at my father caught being the young man I'd never met. It was all true: my old man had lived a life straight out of a Film Noir. I suddenly wished I'd known him then, saw both of us sitting with a couple neat whiskies in the swirling smoke and worn mahogany of the Detroit Press Club talking about the bulldozed juke joints on Hastings Street or the long shadow of the Purple Gang. I wanted to sidekick it with him. I wanted to see what his face looked like by match light in an alley as we fired up a couple Lucky Strikes. I felt gnawed, like I'd blown a chance I'd never even had.

In the photograph, the midget princess is caught forever answering one of my old man's questions. Her mouth is frozen into an O around whatever she's saying, and there's a look of consideration on her face that implies he asked her something worth thinking about. As a reporter in the 1950s, my old man's whole life was focused on asking the right questions. My three older sisters were still little girls at the time, not much bigger than the princess themselves, and my old man had yet to endure those teenage years of, "Since when does midnight mean two in the morning?" or, "Do you actually think I'm letting you leave the house in that skirt?" or any of those one-sided inquiries a father wants his children to answer with obedience, not words. By the time I was in high school, my sisters had already worn down his interest in answers and left to get married. My spiked hair and leather jacket and ripped up jeans, my endless supply of *mans* and *I don't knows*, merited little more than a shake of his head and a snap of the raised front page. But now I'd become uncomfortable with the silence we'd allowed the years to set between us, and there was something about the look on the midget princess's face that made me want to know what he'd asked her at the shutter's instant, as if his question held an answer to the mystery of a father I loved but couldn't say I truly knew.

I put his medals back in the hatbox, returned the hatbox to the shelf, and took the photograph with me into the living room. My old man had levered himself up in his recliner and switched the channel to NASCAR. There he sat in his faded jeans and holey socks, an arm folded across his belly and the tip of his index finger resting reflectively against his lips. My whole life, this was the way I'd seen him relaxing alone. Walking in on him this time, I remembered that more than once over the last few years I'd taken the tip of my finger away from my lips, looked down the length of my dirty jeans at a toe poking through the hole in my tube sock and shaken my head with a smile.

He was unaware of me as I stood a few steps behind his recliner, collecting in my head all I could about the photograph before I asked him about it. What I knew was the obvious—things I could put together through our general family history or see for myself: he was a reporter for the *Detroit Times*; she was a midget princess; the picture was taken at night on the Detroit Metro Airport runway sometime in the late 1950s. Although he was only thirty-something at the time, I noticed that the photograph has him looking kind of stretched out for his age. It's a shot from that era when reporters used to drink their breakfasts at the bar and fight for the phone booth to call copy in to the desks. An era where they would follow a story from the second it broke until it went cold, sometimes sleeping in their cars or living in cut-rate motels for days on end, washing their one pair of socks and underwear in the sink before hanging them on a knocking bathroom radiator to dry. It looked like that kind of living was beginning to wear on my old man, with the skin on his neck starting to wattle and those dark circles blooming under his eyes. Lately, I'd been seeing that same future in my own face when I stared into the bathroom mirror, and I'd just stand there and take it. I'd stand there and let time carve me into my old man. I'd tell him what was on my mind. "Maybe we should have talked more," I'd say as I turned away into the fact that both of us prefer the company of solitude.

I knew that before the picture was taken, my old man had been on the graveyard shift covering car wrecks and fires and rapes and murders and other things gone wrong inside the night. He spent a lot of time with the police. My mother was at home with my three sisters during that time, and it was tough for her, his being away, sometimes for days, only to come back and crash land after he'd banged out these sad stories of human wreckage. But he was a damn good reporter, a natural who could always find the angle, so an editor finally got it right when he must have said, "Moon, you and Flash here head down to the airport and get the scoop on the princess midget for the morning edition."

Which appears to be exactly what they did. A photographer whose name I'll never know and my old man jumped into a beat up press corps car in the middle of the night and drove to Detroit Metro to watch an old yet child-like midget princess walk down the stairs a ground crew had rolled up to that plane. He started asking her questions almost as soon as her feet met the ground, something you can see is true because surrounding the two of them is nothing but runway and darkness and the edge of a gigantic airplane wheel. Then, as my old man was getting his quotes, this photographer snapped a picture so good you could call it "Moon with Princess" and hang it in a gallery or put it in a book. It's that interesting to look at, and Moon is what the other reporters called my old man, a nickname they'd given him because he shared a last name with a newspaper cartoon-strip character most people are too young to remember.

After the princess story ran, the editor kept feeding my old man features, and he started winning awards for his articles. Eventually, they moved him to the day shift, giving him his choice of stories off the Human Interest desk until *The News* and *The Free Press* sucked up all *The Times'* advertising accounts and ran them out of business. After that, everything changed for my family. With his newspaper connections, my old man landed a high profile job doing PR for the auto industry, a job with a much bigger salary that led to a connected life where he traveled the world and powerful automakers like Lee Iacocca and Carol Shelby knew him well. It probably bothered my mom that he was still gone a lot, but she had me, a kid in grade school to keep her busy now that my sisters were in college, and the money he was making meant a better life for all of us, especially when he was around.

I mean I certainly didn't know anyone in my grade school who could brag about being driven around the racetrack at Daytona in a pace car at over 100 miles per hour by a driver who takes his hands off the wheel when you're high up in the fourth turn and about to wet your shorts at the thought of blasting over the lip of the track and off into the sky. My old man was right there, grinning, ready with a physics lesson, "Now *that's* centrifugal force."

Nor was my old man one to mince words or suffer fools. At eighteen, he was floating around the Pacific on a destroyer escort, worrying about torpedoes and kamikazes, following in the shoes of my Uncle Eddie, a Warrant Machinist, and itching to avenge the death of my Uncle John who'd died in the tail gun of a B-17. When I was eighteen I was looking to pick up girls and get loaded at college keg parties, trying not to worry about living up to the man who grew out of that submarine-chasing kid. He understood the predicament I was in, which is why he tried to make me feel better by saying, "Son, you can be anything you want. All I want is for you to be happy. Be a garbage man for all I care. Just be the best one you can."

Standing there, holding a piece of my old man's mythic history, all of these thoughts rattling around, my mind moving back and forth between his past and our now, I could see him coming home early in the morning after that picture was taken and talking with my mother about the princess while she serves him dinner. This was years before I was even an idea. He's eating last night's fried chicken and mashed potatoes and peas as the sunrise begins to push through the slats in the kitchen blinds. My toddler sisters are still asleep upstairs. My mother is leaning against the sink, looking into his tired face, wiping her hands on a dishtowel. "Teresa, her arm isn't much thicker," he says, holding up his drumstick. She just smiles and shakes her head. "Francis," she says, though I'm not sure what she means by this.

But standing there, staring at the back of his graying head, I also knew better. My imagination couldn't change the fact that the man who looked too much like a private detective in that photograph would always be something of a mystery to me. The old man I knew was not the jet-haired reporter crouched beneath an angled fedora asking questions of a midget princess on a dark airport runway. He was a retired white-haired auto exec who spent a good deal of time sitting in a patio chair high up on the balcony of a Florida condo, sipping whiskey and watching waves beat their final purpose against the sand. He was in no hurry to ask questions of anyone or make a point. He rarely even spoke unless spoken to. He was just gazing out at the world's ebb and flow, reading the newspaper and *Autoweek*, taking in sunsets, biding his time. This was my old man, the man of whom I asked, "So what's the story with this?" when I finally stepped forward, touched him on the shoulder, and showed him a photograph.

A few months after I returned from Florida, I landed a job writing for *The Gazette* here in my town. Arts and Entertainment stuff. Film reviews. Wire edits. Captions. Once I had a few decent articles under my belt, the idea that I actually was a reporter sank in, and I got up the guts to tell my old man. "Familiar start," he said, and I agreed. It does feel familiar, like I'm about to get a late-night break where the editor assigns me a midget princess of my own, and sends me off to some backstage Green Room where a staff photographer catches me in the smoke-whorled lamplight, leaning across a bottle-littered coffee table toward a fading rock star, pen against the notepad on my thigh.

That day when I asked my old man about the photograph of the midget princess, I expected to get a reporter's facts: what country she came from, her name, the photographer's name, the year the photograph was taken. Instead I watched his eyes drift over the thing for some time, drawing lines of connection between this image of his former self and an only son who now bore no small resemblance to the reporter on that airport runway. Finally, he spoke.

"What are you doing here?" he asked.

My heart sank. I remembered that we were at the beginning of his long goodbye. I wasn't sure what to say.

He read my face, understood, and smiled. "No. That's the first question I asked her," he said, "What are you doing here?"

He went on to tell me that she was a little woman with a big heart, some kind of European royalty who'd offered up her family's estate for use as an Allied Air Force hospital during World War II. Years after the war, her son had found a wooden box of USAF pilot's wings in the estate's wine cellar, and she'd come to America to personally return them to the Air Force.

"Might as well be you in that shot," my old man said as he handed the photograph back. "Why don't you hold onto that for me." Which is exactly what I did.

I took the photograph with me when I left Florida. I looked at it on the flight home. I looked at it as I put it in a frame. I'm looking at it now, hanging on the wall above the table where I sometimes type my stuff on an old, manual Underwood I bought at the thrift, and I am still unsure what the real story is, what this picture actually says about my myth versus the real old man. Unsure like I sometimes get when I'm trying to do my job, staring at a shot of a pretty woman painting a kid's face at a county fair or a smiling blind man having his hand licked by a seeing eye dog, and I'm unable to find the right caption, those words that see through what's obviously there to tell us what's really inside the picture.

*What are you doing here?* my old man had asked. Meaning, "This is how you question the heart." Meaning, "Here I am twice confronting the ghost of my youth as the son who resembles me holds out a photo from my past." *What are you doing here?* I ask the same thing of our face when I look in the mirror, searching for my angle in that story they'll headline *Son Seeks Truth Behind Father's Mystery by Reading Too Much into Photograph.* A story I will end with the rest of what my old man told me that day I handed him the picture of the midget princess: *Listen. It's no mystery. The real story is never in the fire, but in the way the fire flickers on the faces of the family watching their house burn down. It's not in the car wreck, but in the place the driver left behind and the place he'll never reach. It's not in the fact that the princess was a midget, but in the idea that for her every journey is twice as far. It's not in the spaces that might grow between people, but in the ways we reach across.*

-30-

## The Bachelor's Last Will and Testament

This morning out in front of your apartment on the day before your wedding, feral children do back-flips across the dirty mattress you've junked at the curb. They kick into the air, heels over heads, only to crash and bounce away with the creaking of familiar springs. You watch them from your balcony on the second floor, stirring a Bloody Mary with your finger, remembering that mattress and how you humped it for years all over town, flopping it to the floor of those rented rooms where you've known the women you've known.

This afternoon at the bar you'll sit on a torn barstool bathed in the swirling, dust-moted sunbeam that falls through door's window, making a last supper of seventy-five-cent drafts and a greasy pulled-pork sandwich as you tend the chemical fire in your gut and wonder about your future with *her*. Love aside, you'll drink the beer, pick at the sandwich, and try not to settle on the idea that you're asking too much of yourself.

Come evening you'll get a six to go, sipping the beers as you continue to contribute to the summer's unrest by throwing fireworks down at the street from your apartment window, scattering roaming packs of kids like gravel. You'll blow up every single Black Cat and Lady Finger you have, knowing that once you leave this place, they'll stone these windows wide open, and you'll be the one to blame.

Later, you'll turn off all the lights, pull up the shades and strip out of your clothes. Crank the Alice Cooper then slip on that tux again just to make sure. You'll wear it onto the balcony and drink beer among the potted plants, noting the pointed mother-in-law's tongue. You'll sit on the folding chair, your feet up on the railing as you watch the junk cars come and go from the crack house on the corner.

Around midnight you'll unplug the phone and wish you could prong a hanger between your shoulder blades and step fully tuxed into the closet. Wouldn't they come for you eventually, the best of men, your friends sure as gravity in their own dark suits? By then you'll see the shape of the storm—the gauzy white mist, a hail of rice and baby's breath.

In the end you'll find yourself stretched out on the floor on top of your sleeping bag, surrounded by your life in boxes as you watch the usual sirens bleed red-blue trouble across your apartment's sweaty ceiling. Just before dawn you'll catch the dopplering moan of an a.m. train that sounds exactly like the one still keeping you and a lost love awake in a different city years ago. Unsettled and naked, you'll say a name out loud in the dark then rise to take inventory:

*Being of sound mind and disposing memory, I will awaken one night soon inside another life, listening to two cats pad down the hallways of a new apartment in a better part of town, my job's suit and shoes waiting for the alarm that summons me to rise and fill them. I hereby declare that acting without duress or undue influence during this moment, I will consider old longings as they writhe through my mind then drift away upon the understanding that henceforth there will be moonlight leaking through the bedroom blinds and a summer wind on my wife's skin, a baby growing within her, and in as much as I can devise and bequeath my past to its trustees, I shall make, publish, and swear this document to be my Last Will and Testament, thereby revoking any and all others.*

## Steam

Walking his little daughter to the city playground on a cool-bright October afternoon, he notices the steam smoking through Detroit's manholes, steam lisping from curbside sewer mouths edged with the sparkling grit of broken glass.

His daughter notices, too.

"What's that, Daddy," she asks, demanding an explanation of steam at three years old.

"That's steam," he says.

"Steam," she echoes, considering the word and the fact of steam for the first time as far as he knows.

He tries to think of how to best explain steam to a three-year old. "It happens when you boil water. It's kind of like mist. It's there and not there," he says for lack of a simpler explanation. Then he thinks of the scalding, "But sometimes it can burn you, so you have to be really careful around it."

She's ignored the second part, of course. "Steam!" his daughter shouts, starting to skip, her little hand swallowed in his, "Steam, steam, steam, steam, steam!"

Once they hit the playground she's forgotten all about steam. What she wants now is the swing. She requires pushing, not his oversimplifications.

"Faster," she says. "Higher."

He sends her out and gathers her in, getting caught up in her excitement and happiness as he feels her body's imprint touch his hands and leave again and again.

"Higher," she wants to go, "Higher!" And with one push he sends her too high for their own good because the chains twist and his heart knocks against his ribs as she swings crazily for a second, scaring herself and him before she begins to cry.

He quickly reins the swing in, scoops her up, sees over the top of her head to the lean boys playing basketball on the park's nearby court, one rising now toward the rim. He feels a small tug on his T-shirt; his daughter is pulling him back. Wonder has wiped away her fear.

"Look." She whispers the magic of her discovery, pointing at her footprint in the sand beneath the settling swing, "I was there, and now I'm not."

He swallows the difficult truth, the fact that at three years old she has already begun to understand impact and leaving, longing's proof that love and distance mean someone can be there and not be there at the same time in a way that somehow burns. Like steam. Then his selfish reflection breaks open and becomes bittersweet. She's realized the first step toward a life and future of her own; she's reminded him that to love her means he will have to pay out line and let her go.

Later, he rides her home on his shoulders while she points out everything she sees. "Bus!" she says when one breezes by. "Birdie!" And he looks up just as the dark, backlit silhouette leaps from a tall building's edge into the wind.

# II

# DISCHORDS

*There are people in this audience with broken bones,*
*others whose bones will break sooner or later,*
*people who've ruined their health, worshipped their own lies,*
*spat on their dreams, turned their backs on their true beliefs,*
*yes, yes, and all will be saved. All will be saved. All will be*
*saved.*

Denis Johnson, *Tree of Smoke*

## Shots

It was his thirtieth birthday party and he'd cooked a pot-ful of chili for the party of friends who were drinking at his place. All evening he'd been putting down shots of whiskey from a little glass shot-mug, a gift from his girlfriend with his name etched into a circle of pewter on one side. "So no matter how drunk I get, I still know who I am," he kept saying when he'd show it off to someone he hadn't shown it to yet. "Happy birthday," they'd say, clinking their glass against his little mug of whiskey before they drank.

Around midnight, hours after the chili was gone and he was thoroughly drunk, he got on the drum kit set up in the basement of the house they rented and started jamming improvisational jazzrockcountryfunk fusion, one friend on the bass, a few others on guitar. Though he was actually a guitar player, he liked to consider himself a "closet drummer." Over the years, he'd taught himself the basics on the practice kits the drummers in his various bands had kept set up in his place, and he'd gotten pretty good. There was a loose, childish freedom in his playing, something he never found on the guitar, and he especially liked to play when he was drunk, for the way it would cause him to get lost in the beat and forget himself.

Down in his basement, they started trying to take the music places, and he lead the way, syncopating heavily, playing ahead of the beat or playing behind, occasionally tripping off into half-times then boiling his way into 4/4 with a tight snare roll which seamlessly snapped them back into the original signature. He kept at it, inspired though irregular in his rhythms, looking for that egoless place inside the music, until he slipped so deep into the swirl of sound that something came loose inside. The whiskey spins had finally found him. Lurching up, he staggered out from behind the kit and bumped his way through the party, the faces of his friends swimming past him on his way to the front door.

A cold night, December in the Midwest, dramatic black-blue shadows thrown across the glittering crust of snow by floodlights. He did not truly feel the cold and so stepped outside in just his jeans and T-shirt, sobering slightly in the cooler air. He heard the front door opening behind him, and, for no conscious reason, took off running toward the end of his long driveway. He slid to a stop where the shoveled driveway hit the slushy street and squinted back at the waving silhouette standing in the doorway surrounded by a halo of laughter and light. It was probably his girlfriend, though he couldn't tell for certain. He waved an exaggerated wave in return then started walking down the plowed street lined by mounds of snow.

He was breathing heavily from his short run, the cold air pepperminting his lungs. He hooked his fingers behind his neck and tilted his head back as he walked. Many stars spun against the cloudless winter night. A lot of his favorite people were inside, and he'd had too many shots to be able to talk sensibly with any of them. It occurred to him then that he'd done this a number of times before, gotten wasted early and missed out. It was the shots. Belly up against the counter of some bar, or drinking in his own house, it was always the shots that did this to him, firing his mind, filling him with the heat of these poignant moments he kept hoping to pin down with more whiskey, only to find he'd blurred the outlines of his life and forgotten, one drink at a time, each thing he'd wanted so badly to remember.

He staggered a step, steadied himself, shook his head hard to clear it. Everything up and down the block was frosted with snow, and the streetlights pressed sharp shadows onto the picturesque Victorian houses. He'd always liked this old neighborhood: big lawns, lots of old trees, the gingerbread homes with their ornate woodwork on the eaves and porches. The rent was reasonable, too. Mostly because they were only a block or so away from the north side of town where things could quickly get dangerous.

A pair of headlights swung around the corner onto his street. He blinked in the glare, slipped a little on a slick patch of packed snow as he tried to focus on the approaching vehicle. More friends were expected, even at this hour. The black Cherokee rolled up next to him and stopped. The tinted window behind the driver hummed down, revealing someone in a rubber Jimmy Carter mask pointing a pistol at him.

"Ka-blam!" Jimmy said, and laughed a muffled laugh.

He was so drunk he barely reacted. The mask swam. He squinted. Swayed. Tried to steady himself.

"Hey there," he said, unsure if he knew the people inside. "Whassup?"

"Man, look at you getting your party on," Jimmy said. More laughter, this time from people he couldn't see, drifted out of the Cherokee, and he caught a whiff of weed. "You know where 713 is, bro?" Jimmy asked.

He tried to work the idea of which houses had what numbers through his head. It wasn't happening. He got disoriented and felt suddenly dizzy.

"Um. Maybe down that way, I think." He waved a loose arm toward the other end of the block.

"Alright then. Hey, you have a few more for me, my man."
More laughter. The tinted window slid back up, and the car
drove on slowly, its tires creaking against the snow.

Back inside, the heat and noise and people at the party were
unbearable. He stumbled into the kitchen, leaned up against
the wall near the refrigerator as the room hurled itself upon
itself. His girlfriend's face briefly came into focus. He felt her
hand on his cheek.

"Man, you're wasted," she said, "You should go lay down."

He grunted at her, staggered out of the kitchen and into the
smoky living room, bumping through the loud, well-lubed
crowd as he made his way toward the ratty recliner. He didn't
want to give up on the night and go to bed. He wasn't sure if he
could make it that far anyway. Maybe he could rally. He flopped
down into the chair, levered up the footrest, leaned the seat
back, took a look around the swimming room and passed out.

Some time later he woke up confused to the sound of sirens.
All his friends were gone. Empty cans and bottles covered every
flat surface in the room. Someone had taken off his shoes and
socks and written *Love* and *Hate* across the tops of his bare feet
in black magic marker. He didn't notice this as he pushed
himself up and staggered to the bathroom, tongue dry as gauze,
his pounding head whining in slashes like it was filled with a
gyroscope tipped in razorblades. He slammed a glass of water,
retched, tossed in aspirin and more water until, finally, his
mind separated and made sense of the sirens, which were
louder now and varied: fire trucks, police cars, ambulances—it
seemed as if a squadron of each were blaring down his street
when, abruptly, all the noise cut off.

Fingers of one hand pressed against his temples, he made his way to the living room window and looked out. An ambulance, two fire trucks and five police cars were clustered at the end of his block, their red-blue lights splashing color across the snow and ornate houses. Smoke poured from the second story of a house near the corner. Firemen quickly unrolled hoses. He stood at the edge of the curtain, watching flame lick out the house's windows, feeling as if there was some reason for him to shrink away from being seen. He belched whiskey then turned from the window, suddenly overcome by the idea that something was missing, that someone he didn't know had shown up after he'd passed out and taken a record or a knick-knack or an instrument cable. He looked around at the disaster that was his living room, staring blankly, his head throbbing to his body's anguished pulse, and he remembered he'd been having a dream before the sirens awakened him—a dream of a door slamming sharply two or three times. Looking down, he noticed the backwards words written in marker across the tops of his bare feet. He went and sat on the couch to try and make out what they said.

Sitting there, lost somewhere between drunk and sick, holding the *Love* foot in his lap, he knew that some important piece of the evening had been lost to him, but the question of who had written on his feet and the sound and image of the dream door slamming had forced whatever that loss was from his mind. He sat dumbly on the living room couch for some time, foot cradled in his lap, siren lights pulsing across the ceiling, brain firing and misfiring fragments of the night through his head. Down the hall, he could barely make out his girlfriend, asleep, her back turned toward the open bedroom door. Eventually, he noticed the sky begin to pale, and he stood up on uneasy legs, gnawed by the vague regret that there was something worth remembering he'd forgotten.

## Guilty

Stork had just finished smoking a joint when he thought he heard someone knocking on the front door. He was in his bathrobe and boxers, down in the basement practice space of the house he rented with his girlfriend, Heather, a bit hung over and trying to get it together. His band, The Reprobates, was gigging that night at The Wet Spot, a local bar, and there were hours to kill before sound-check. So he'd gotten stoned and started organizing, bagging the empties, unwinding the spaghetti of microphone cords and instrument cables in the middle of the floor. He'd been rolling a few riffs around in his head, thinking about maybe plugging in his guitar and writing some new material, which he liked to do stoned, when he thought maybe he heard someone knocking, but being stoned, he wasn't sure. Then he heard the knocking again, more insistent this time. It wouldn't be Heather. She was out hitting up her friends for "gently used" clothes to bring to Second Chance, her sister Shelby's resale clothing store, and that usually took her a few hours. And she wouldn't knock anyway. Unless she'd lost her key. Again.

Stork went upstairs and cracked open the front door onto cold December. There stood the exterminator, his smoky breath visible in the chilly air.

"Hey, buddy," the exterminator puffed, rubbing his hands together, his face flushed above his tan Orkin coveralls and jacket, which was unzipped and had the name *Bob* stitched in red cursive thread across the left breast. He was a tall, robust, middle-aged man, maybe ten or fifteen years older than Stork with the look of someone who'd worked his share of construction or manual labor. A man who knew how to fix a car and was handy with power tools.

"I was just wondering if I could do your service today," Bob said.

Stork rubbed his stubbly cheek and ran a hand through his messy, shoulder-length hair. It was three in the afternoon, and he had yet to shower, having only been up for an hour or so. When had they signed up for Orkin? Maybe it was something Heather or the landlord had done. He hadn't done it. Or had he? Suddenly, he realized how stoned he was. Were his eyes cashed? Did his breath and clothes reek? Had the smell made it all the way upstairs from the basement? He'd been smoking the dank.

Fantastic, sinister thoughts began to flash through Stork's mind. What if the exterminator was a cop? Or on probation even? Stork knew a dude doing three to five upstate because he left the cable guy in his house during an installation while he went to the grocery store. The cable guy, who also happened to be up on possession charges, discovered the dude's grow room and rolled over on him in exchange for leniency. Then the cops spun the story like the dude was some kind of kingpin, claiming they got him for fifty pounds. Stork knew the truth: five measly plants. A couple ounces of personal smoke at most. Fifty pounds. Sure. If you weighed the stalks and the dirt and the pots.

Stork wasn't so stupid as to leave anyone in his house alone, not with thousands of dollars of music gear in his basement.

But what if this guy was a cop, or was hooked to the cops somehow? Zero Tolerance laws the way they were, that wet stub of a roach sitting in the ashtray on top of his amp downstairs meant they could clean him out, take all his equipment—his '66 Fender Telecaster, the Twin Reverb amp, the PA. Everything. That's what they'd done to that dude, taken every single thing he owned right down to his homemade tie-died tapestries and his espresso maker.

Maybe he should just say no, not today, tell the guy he was heading out right now, do the bug spraying some other time. They couldn't bust him if he didn't let them in, could they? Well, at least not until they came back with a warrant—unless this guy had a warrant and was bluffing for some reason before serving it. But why would he bluff if he had a warrant? Were they trying to sweat him to get to Ron, his dealer? That wasn't going to accomplish much. Stork had no idea where Ron got his weed and he knew better than to ask. And Stork himself certainly wasn't any kind of bust; he never had more than an ounce in the house and usually not even that. They'd never waste the money and time on such a low-profile arrest. But what if someone had lied about him, said he was growing or dealing. But who would do...

Bob cleared his throat. "Everything okay, buddy? I can come back later if there's a problem," he said.

Stork snapped to. Saying no would look even more suspicious. "No, no, that's cool," he said. "How long will it take?"

Bob shrugged, made a face that suggested this wasn't the kind of question he was used to getting. "I don't know, about twenty minutes, I guess."

"Okay," Stork said, "Let me go throw some clothes on first."

"Either way," Bob said, and Stork noticed the man was looking beyond him, surveying the living room.

"That oak paneling you got there?" Bob asked, nodding past him.

"Yeah, I think so," Stork said, but he had no idea what kind of paneling it was or how to tell the difference between one kind of wood and another.

"Nice," Bob said, nodding his head, appraising something. "Well, I'll go get my gear." He turned and walked down the haphazardly shoveled front walk to his black truck with its tinted windows and big red and white ORKIN sign on the door.

Stork scanned the living room to make sure there was no paraphernalia in sight. His three foot water bong was standing in the corner next to the stereo speaker, not obviously out in the open, but certainly there for someone to notice if they knew what they were looking for. He grabbed the bong and opened the closet door. The closet was filled with trash bags of the clothing Heather constantly cycled in and out of the house. Things were getting a bit out of hand on that front. Between the clothes Heather brought home and all these other chicks he barely knew dropping stuff off, their closets were pretty much stuffed. It annoyed the hell out of Stork, but it was a good gig in theory: Heather gave the chicks a little slice of cash for their used clothes, which she then brought down to Second Chance for Shelby to sell at a higher price so the two of them could split the profits.

Stork lifted a bag out of the way, shoved the bong into the back of the closet and set the bag back down in front of it, spilling a little bongwater in the process. He made a quick sweep of his bedroom as he threw on some clothes and found nothing more incriminating than a scattering of Heather's dirty underwear, which he kicked under the bed. Then he went into the bathroom, grabbed the air-freshener spray from under the sink and sprayed a trail along the hallway and down the basement stairs into the practice space the band had sectioned off by hanging up blankets and strips of eggshell foam. He set the spray down on top of his amp, ate the roach in the ashtray then tapped the ashes from the ashtray into an empty beer can. "Just the exterminator," he told himself, "Guy doesn't give a shit if you smoke a little weed."

But what if Ron had gotten pegged and rolled over and turned in all his customers to shave some time off a possession charge? Lately, weird things had been going on with Stork's landline: hang-up calls, single rings then nothing. A few friends had openly asked him to get bags for them on the line, and he'd agreed. Did that make him a dealer even though he didn't make any profit on the deal? Stork took a few deep breaths to try and steady himself and walked back up the basement stairs, sniffing for the stink of weed beneath the cloying scent of air freshener.

When he opened the basement door and stepped into the kitchen, he was surprised to see Bob there, coat off, down on his knees in front of the counter holding a spray can with a long, thin nozzle.

"You seen much action around here lately?" he asked Stork, then looked back to his work, pressing down on the can's top to squeeze a clear line of some chemical into the cracks between the cabinets and the tile floor. Stork noticed Bob's large hands. The fine spider webs of dirt worked deeply into the wrinkles of his fingers had a look of permanence to them. A fading U.S.M.C. tattoo of an eagle sitting on top of the anchored world covered his thick forearm.

"No. Just the occasional ant."

"Interesting," Bob said.

"Yeah. Guess we need to sweep more."

"Most do."

Stork took in the kitchen with its pile of dirty dishes in the sink and caught sight of the small silver pipe next to the microwave. A tingly shock of fear shot through him. Goddamn

Heather, getting stoned before doing dishes she doesn't finish. He nonchalantly grabbed a dishrag and ran it across the counter, over to the microwave, palming the pipe as the rag covered it. He looked up and noticed Bob watching him.

"Sorry about the mess. My girl isn't much for keeping house."

"Amazing how things can pile up on you without your realizing it," Bob said.

Stork nodded and kept nodding. "Yep. Yep. I hear that." He wadded the rag tightly in his hand. "Well, I guess I'll leave you to it," he said as he went to the basement door. "I'll be downstairs if you need me."

"Okay then," Bob said, "I'll get you when I'm ready."

In the basement, Stork hid the pipe in his guitar case, sprayed another round of air freshener and tried to finish untangling the wad of instrument cables and microphone cords piled in the middle of the floor as he wondered what Bob meant. *I'll get you when I'm ready?* What the hell did that mean? Was this guy a cop or what? Had Bob seen the pipe before Stork palmed it? Had he seen the bong? Did it even matter? Was Stork in the middle of getting busted, or was this just Bob, the Orkin Man, spraying his place for bugs? He imagined Bob coming into the basement, gun drawn, to tell him game over. No way was Stork going to jail. He'd have to go for the gun, grapple with Bob. Use the butt to knock him out. He'd gag him with duct tape, tie his legs and arms with guitar cables, then run back up the stairs and try to make it to the car for a getaway. Only to have cops all up and down the street springing out from behind bushes and trees. Cop cars screeching up to blockade the intersections. Cops in flack jackets with DEA painted on the back. Buzz-headed, thick-necked cops with shotguns screaming "Freeze, you fuck," before they pumped him full of bullets because they'd decided to take his raising his hands in surrender as some kind of threat. He threw down the tangle of cables in frustrated disgust at both himself and the world.

The basement door opened and Stork heard the exterminator clomping down the stairs in his work boots. He stood frozen behind the wall of blankets, his breathing short and tight as if even thinking he'd been caught at something illegal would get him busted. *Fuck all this wondering*, he told himself, and swept the curtain of hanging blankets aside to face the music.

"Well, I've finished servicing the upstairs," Bob said. "Kitchen, living room, bedroom. Your hallway closet. Man, that thing is packed tight. What's with all those trash bags?"

Stork's guts wrenched. Why had he said it that way, leaving the closet until last, emphasizing it like that? "So what if I like a to smoke pot," he wanted to yell, "I try to be a decent person. What about your goddamn alcohol, man? Your drunk drivers? Your drunken murders?" But Stork knew he had to ride this one out, whatever it brought. Just play it cool.

"Nothing. Old clothes. My girlfriend's stuff," he said, "Anything else you need to do?"

Bob didn't appear to be listening. Or maybe he was ignoring Stork on purpose, Stork couldn't tell. He watched as Bob sniffed the air deeply a few times then started walking the basement's perimeter, stooping or stretching now and then to spray a line of chemicals into the crevices where the walls met the floor or up toward the exposed beams of the ceiling. It all seemed so haphazard, less like Bob was spraying for insects and more like he was looking for something.

"Smells like you got a mold problem going on down here," Bob said after he'd made a circuit of the walls. "Termites love that moisture. They'll eat your joists out, send your whole world crashing down on you."

"Well, I wouldn't really know," Stork said, "I just moved here in September. I only rent this place."

"What you got going on in there?" Bob walked quickly over to the blankets closing off the center of the room and swept one aside with an arm. "Whew, look at all that stuff. You a musician or something, buddy?"

"Yeah, I'm in a rock band, we play around the area."

"Man, must be nice not having to do the daily grind. Get to party all the time."

"It's not like that," Stork said, "It's a lot of work, actually, writing material, practicing, promoting, booking shows, driving there and back, loading in, loading out. The time you spend playing is probably the only good thing about it. It's not like we're famous or anything. Most of us have day jobs. At least for now."

"So you got today off then," Bob said.

"Well, no. I do all the booking and promotion for the band. I write most of the songs, too. That's a full time job."

"You're a songwriter, huh," Bob said, looking Stork up and down, taking in the long hair and earrings, the stained ratty jeans and flannel shirt. "You like Hank?"

"Who?"

"Move it on Over. Your Turn to Cry. Drifting Too Far From the Shore."

"What?"

"Hank, man. Hank Williams Senior, the greatest country musician and songwriter of all time. Least I think so."

"Oh, Hank. Yeah, I listen to him now and then."

"Oh, that's right," Bob said dismissively, "You boys play that rock stuff."

And despite it all, Stork actually felt a little twinge of hurt at the way he'd seemingly just gone down a few notches in the man's opinion.

"You know you might wanna try learning some Hank," Bob said, "Goes over big in every bar I ever been in."

"I bet," Stork said. He was still nervous, but he now doubted Bob was an informer or a cop. He seemed too genuine with his stocky build and hair graying at the temples, with his scuffed boots and his tan uniform. He was obviously a man's man who'd worked his whole life and probably liked to toss back a few beers while watching the game. He was no different from most guys Stork knew, working his job, just trying to get by.

"I'll talk to the band about it," Stork said.

Bob simply nodded, and suddenly Stork wanted him to understand that he'd done his share of man's work, too. He'd had his landscaping jobs and his janitor's job's and his assembly line jobs. All that dead end shit. He didn't want Bob thinking he was some lazy-ass, dope-smoking musician who flopped around all day while real people were out working. He'd spent almost ten years learning how to play the guitar. And now he could shred, man. He'd worked hard to get this band up and going, spent hours every day on the phone promoting, and The Reprobates were doing okay, filling the clubs, pulling in four to six hundred a gig, gigging two, sometimes three, nights a week around the state. People were starting to notice, too. If the band stayed at it long enough, worked hard enough, and he kept writing good songs, they just might get signed. Maybe. It was a risk worth taking for a dream.

"So what's that stuff you were spraying?" Stork asked.

"FICAM-DUST," Bob said, looking at the can as if he needed to read the label. "Good stuff, takes care of spiders and ants."

Stork remembered the spider he'd plucked off the kitchen ceiling the night before. A big spider he'd held gently in a tissue and set free into the winter darkness, even though afterwards he'd realized the thing must have frozen solid within a minute of being let outside. It probably would have been more humane to have crushed it dead on the spot.

"Yeah? You know, now that I think about it, I did see a big spider on the kitchen ceiling the other night, and a few weeks before that I saw a couple in the bathroom, and one in the bedroom."

"Thought you said it was just ants."

"I guess I forgot about the spiders until you mentioned them."

"You got an attached garage, right?"

"Yeah. But there's no way into it from inside the house. It's weird."

"Probably an addition, " Bob said. "That's not unusual. I should get in there and take a look around."

They went back up into the kitchen, where Bob shrugged into his Orkin coat and Stork slipped on his boots, took his keys off the hook, and led the way outside.

The afternoon sun was bright on the snow, and Stork's eyes smarted against the glare. As they crunched across the frozen footprints that made a path toward the garage door, he began to wonder how much Bob actually knew about insects. Getting stoned and watching those insect shows on cable was one of his favorite things to do, even though he never really held on to many of the facts.

"I think it was a wolf spider," Stork said as he unlocked the garage door then slid it up on its tracks.

"What?" Bob snapped his eyes away from the street.

"I said I think maybe it was a wolf spider I saw on the kitchen ceiling the other night."

"Could be," Bob said, and he walked into the garage with his little spray can of FICAM.

Stork stood in the mouth of the garage, watching Bob move quickly in the dimness at the back, squirting FICAM here and there.

"What other kinds of spiders like to get inside?" Stork asked.

Bob seemed annoyed. "Any kind wants to get away from the cold, I suppose."

Stork felt ridiculous for asking what he knew was a stupid question. The guy obviously wasn't a cop or an informant, but he'd probably seen that pipe or the bong and now had Stork pegged as some kind of burned-out half-wit, and that was bullshit. Maybe he did smoke pot every day, but his mind was still as sharp as anybody's. He just couldn't seem to think of anything interesting to say right now. He tried to remember some unusual fact he'd learned about insects on one of those nature shows, but dung beetles rolling balls of shit and the general deception and devouring of the insect world were the only things that came to mind.

"I read somewhere black widows like garages," Stork said, finally.

"Yep, and basements and attics, too, like most spiders. They like it in the corners. Somewhere safe where they can see what's coming at them."

"Yeah, the corners," Stork said, "You're absolutely right. That's where I saw the spider in the kitchen."

It was funny, now that he thought about it, Heather's whole freakout last night. Something a guy like Bob might appreciate.

"Man, she went nuts. I was in the basement working on a tune and I hear her upstairs screaming bloody murder, 'Oh my god, oh my god!' and I come running up thinking she's hurt or someone's broken in or whatever, and there she is all crouched down near the fridge pointing up at this big ol' spider camped out in the corner of the ceiling. So I get a plastic cup and climb up on a chair and the spider starts jumping around like a goddamn rabbit before I can catch it and let it outside. I mean it was really hard to catch it without killing it. But I got that mother. It was a bitch, but I got him."

Bob stopped spraying and turned to Stork. "You let it out? Why didn't you squash the damn thing?"

"I don't know. I guess I don't like killing spiders if I can avoid it. Every time I see one I think of this haiku I read: 'Don't worry spiders, I keep house casually.'"

"A haiku?"

"Yeah, it's a short Japanese poem. This one was by some guy Basho, I think."

"I know what a haiku is," Bob said. "That doesn't seem long enough to be a haiku."

"I think it was in a book of haikus," Stork said, "Maybe not. I don't remember."

"Huh. Don't worry spiders," Bob said, "Glad most people don't think that way. I'd be out of a job." He sprayed a few more haphazard shots of FICAM then straightened up and walked over to Stork standing in the mouth of the garage.

"Well, that about does it," he said, then pulled a cell phone that looked more like a little walkie-talkie out of the inside pocket of his coat.

Stork's stomach jumped up into his chest.

"Service Seven to Office One," Bob said, "I'm finished with my last client. Heading in."

"Ten four, seven. You're logged. Get a signature. Out."

"Will do. Out."

Stork's heart pounded. A film of sweat burst out hot and quickly cooled against his back as Bob reached inside his coat again.

"Got something for you," Bob said.

Holy shit. How could he have been so stupid? Stork flashed on the idea of leaping back and slamming down the garage door between them, trapping Bob inside as he made a run for it.

Bob pulled out a folded set of papers that looked something like an oversized ticket with its three different colored sheets attached at the top, and he handed the papers to Stork. Hands shaking, Stork could barely unfold it. Out of the corner of his eye, Stork saw Bob rooting around in his pocket for something else, probably cuffs or a gun. Bob's hand came out with a pack of Camel no filters. He shook one out and lipped it, then stood staring at Stork.

"Oh, sorry about that," Bob said. His hand went inside his coat again and came out with a pen.

Stork's swimming eyes cleared. He was holding a bill for the Orkin service.

Bob set down the can of FICAM on top of the trash bin and lit his cigarette. He held the pack out to Stork.

"You smoke," Bob said more than asked.

Stork shook his head no.

"Thought for sure you did," Bob said, "Being a musician and all." He tucked the pack away. "Yep, you're about my last service for the day." He took a drag and jetted the smoke out through his nose. "Got to get on over to my daughter's and help her pack her stuff. She's going off to school at Michigan State. No thanks to me or my ex, though. She busted her butt all through high school, that girl. Got herself a academic scholarship."

Bob picked a flake of tobacco off his tongue, looked at it, and flicked it away.

"Just put the payment down on a used Escort for her the other day," he said. "Now she can come and go how she wants. All her friends out partying, drinking and getting knocked up and shit." He looked Stork dead in the eye. "Smoking that dope. They're going no place fast. I feel sorry for their parents. It's like some people never learn what's really important in life, you know what I'm saying?"

Whatever was going on, Stork had had enough. He signed the bill without reading and handed it back. Now that he wanted Bob gone, Bob seemed to have nothing but time.

"She's about the best daughter a father could ask for, I'll tell you what. Her mother though, phffff, who knows what the hell I was thinking there."

Bob looked out from the mouth of the garage toward the street as he peeled the top sheet off the bill and handed it back to Stork. "Say, what time does your lady get home?"

"What the fuck does your daughter or my girlfriend have to do with anything?" Stork snapped.

"Jesus, buddy," Bob said, "Only making conversation. No need to get all tore up."

Stork could barely hold Bob's eye. He fought down the trembling in his legs.

"Just go, man. Please," he said.

"Whatever you say. *Sir.*"

Folding the papers into his pocket, Bob grabbed his can of FICAM off the trash bin and walked a few steps out of the garage. Then he stopped short and turned back to face Stork. He reached up with his index finger and pulled down the skin just below his right eye. Stork saw the red, moist flesh beneath the eyeball before Bob let the skin snap up again. He pulled his hand away, cocked the finger like a gun at Stork.

"You seem like a pretty good kid," he said, "You ought to keep an eye. You never know what's creeping around in your house." He turned to go. A garbled voice came over the phone in his pocket.

Right then, Heather pulled up into the driveway in her beat to shit Dodge Colt. She stepped out, her paisley skirt and long black hair swinging. She looked at Bob suspiciously.

"Afternoon, ma'am," Bob said.

"Who's this?" Heather asked Stork.

"Orkin guy," Stork mumbled, feeling his legs go weaker.

Just then a police cruiser with its lights flashing but its sirens off pulled up and blocked the end of Stork's driveway.

Bob walked to his truck and stood there as Stork leaned against the trash bin to keep from falling over. Two plainclothes cops got out of the cruiser and walked quickly up the drive.

"Heather Stoyka?" one of them asked.

"What the fuck is going on?" Heather said, "I didn't do anything."

"I'm going to have to ask you to open the trunk of your car, ma'am," the other said.

Stork sat on the front steps of the house. Hot clothes. Hot clothes. It was unbelievable. Heather was a fence for a ring of shoplifters running hot clothes through her sister's second hand store. Images of the bust kept playing in his head. Heather crying, getting cuffed against the hood of the cop car. Heather yelling at Stork to snap the fuck out of it and call her sister, call her mother, call a fucking lawyer. Heather screaming and fighting as they shoved her into the back seat. Bob, watching it all from the side before peeling off the Orkin magnet from his truck door, tossing it into the back and driving away with a shake of his head.

The last of the sun dipped behind the houses across the street. A headache circling his temples, Stork found himself craving a few bong rips. Then Heather's contorted face flashed through his mind again, and he was gripped by self-loathing.

"What the fuck is wrong with you!" He shouted it at the sky, even as he meant it for himself, then he dropped his head, cradling his skull in his hands, his elbows propped on his knees as he pitched a heavy sigh of disgust.

No. He lifted his head. This was Heather's fault. This had nothing to do with him, or with weed. Heather stealing and lying was the problem. Heather living a double life right under his nose. Heather nearly getting *him* busted. That was the problem. Not his smoking. He was a mellow dude. Weed kept him mellow. Kept him even. Made him more thoughtful.

Shit. That roach he'd eaten earlier was the last of his bag. He'd have to go see Ron... but Heather... goddamn it... need money to throw her bail... pay for a lawyer... wait... there was always court-appointed...

Stork stood up.

No way could he keep a bag around while she's waiting for trial though... someone in the band... Leon... Leon could hold... doesn't smoke... won't pinch...

He left the stairs and headed for his car parked at the curb... getting colder fast... busted heater, man... definitely going to need a coat... and your wallet, stoner...

He turned back toward the house.

Images of visiting Heather in prison... talking to her on a skuzzy, black plastic phone... hands pressed up against glass... court-appointed lawyer was a bad idea... maybe Ron could front a pound... flipping it might cover legal fees... get her probation...

He turned back toward the car.

...Okay, so no more weed in the house, ever, not even during practice... stash it outside somewhere in plastic wrap... a hassle having nowhere to weigh and bag, though... all that back and forth...

He stopped and fingered the keys in his pocket.

...Surveillance...

There was no point risking getting fucked over when she's fucked either way... better to just leave... grab the guitar and amp... some clothes... always did want to try L.A.... get the rest of the band to move out there...

He started toward the house again.

...but just ditching her like that...not cool...maybe ask Ron to front a sympathy bag...think over the next move-...maybe she could jump bail and they could disappear together...either way, need a bag for the road.

Stork turned back around and walked to his car. He stuck the key in the door but didn't unlock it. He'd been backed into a corner, felt trapped and stared at, his mind jumping around, trying to find a way to escape the hand of circumstance while seeing a thousand different futures through too many eyes. Frozen, misfiring, wiped blank, he stood there waiting for instinct to reveal an opening. The gray-white gauze of the early winter evening pressed down on him. And he was feeling colder, much colder, the cold so cold it was starting to seem warm.

## Highway Coda

The band drives southbound on a deserted two-lane highway
in their rust-eaten van. In back a dismembered trap kit, black
instrument cases stacked. Hungover, they're rattling like reverb
springs, drifting on bald tires beneath the March sky's gray
wash. Last night three of the four crashed in the cocktail
waitress's living room. Singer, always the charmer, got the bed.
Now they thumb a joint around while Singer drives and maps
the waitress's body for the others, pausing only when he notices
the whitish blur just ahead in the road. "Hey, man," he points,
"dinner." Drummer, shotgun, pulls out a sharpie, adds a mark
to the back of the set list they've duct taped to the dash: one
more roadkill for the running tally they're keeping on this tour.
Closer, they realize it's no possum, but a small, white pint
container of take-out Chinese sitting upright in the center of the
road, lid neatly closed. Even the thin metal handle is raised.
Singer lines up to mow it down, thinking to spray the asphalt
with pork or chicken. The others lean in, anticipate the beat of
the tire against the box, when what they see next sounds like
this: a crow dropping through the air, disappearing into the
blank space before the van's cracked grille. The crow rising
again, flashing across their windshield and pulsing away upon
the flattened light with a downbeat of wings, take-out clasped

by the metal handle swinging in its talons. A black note fading across the smeared page of afternoon.

The coda to last night's show scored onto their brains.

# The Dog in Me

What I thought I needed was a good-looking dog. There were a number of potentials at the shelter, but when they told me Otto couldn't speak, he was a lock. Handsome as the Boxer and the Doberman were, there was no way around it: a silent and obedient pure-bred German Shepherd was exactly what the plan called for.

"Hasn't made a sound since they brought him in," the vet said when I asked if it was true. "We're pretty sure he's mute. Happens sometimes."

"But he's such a good-wooking boy," the vet's attractive female assistant cooed as she crouched before the dog, scratching him behind the ears with a rough attention that had his leg and tail twitching uncontrollably. "Widdle baby is going to a good home. Yes he is."

"He's perfect," I said, taking hold of the business end of his leash.

"So you're getting him neutered, right?" the vet asked.

"We'll have to see," I said, "I'm thinking of doing some breeding."

I signed the papers, paid the fees, brought the dog home. The name Otto was my idea. It seemed fitting. Teutonic. Appropriate for the strong, silent type, and what's not to like about a palindrome?

Over the next few weeks I worked to gain his trust. Early morning walks. Evenings lounging on the cool patio with our legs splayed, scratching ourselves. Weekend afternoons chasing the ball and stick. He seemed to be a good fit. He came when I called. He stayed when I said stay. By all appearances he was an intelligent and loyal dog, despite his being oddly, almost ominously, silent.

One Saturday afternoon after a few beers, I decided he was ready to hear the plan. I was having trouble working up the guts to ask out the woman next door. I'd recently seen her fawning over some stranger's half-breed husky. Otto, with his sleek lines and sharp features, blew that mutt away. He was going to be my in.

The plan was simple enough. Next time I saw my neighbor out watering her flowers in her short shorts and bikini top, I'd put Otto into action. Parade him casually by. Let him work the cute. Nudge him to flutter those big brown eyes and give her that floppy tongued smile. To make sure he truly understood what was at stake, I even showed him my view of things, inching my bedroom curtain aside to reveal her sunbathing in her back yard. Otto licked his nose, gave a toothy yawn, and went right on panting in appreciation. He was on board. All we needed now was an opportunity.

Then one evening, after getting home from the office, I opened my mailbox and saw someone had scribbled *CREEP* on the brown paper wrapper covering my latest issue of *Juggs*. This was upsetting news. Who thought I was a creep? Why? I'd only bought the house that spring. I had yet to introduce myself to any of my neighbors.

There was a possibility. I pictured the bearded, pot-bellied mailman leaning on the chain-link fence surrounding my yard. He's been having a hard time stuffing the bills and *Soldier of Fortune* and *Computer's Monthly* and *The Nation* and my latest issue of *Juggs* into the mailbox when he notices Otto sprawled in the shade of the maple, tongue lolling, his tail thumping the dry lawn as he glances between the binoculars he's taken from my bedroom and my sunbathing neighbor. The dog sees the mailman, trots up to him, sets down the binoculars in his jaws. The mailman is curious to know if what I'd previously told him about Otto being mute is true, so he leans toward the dog's intelligent, brown eyes.

"Hey, boy. Ruff. Ruff. Speak. Speak."

Otto looks at mailman. Looks at the girl. Looks at the binoculars, nudges them with his nose. Again at the mailman. Again at the girl. Again with the binoculars. He might as well have come out and said it: *He's spying on that hot bitch next door.*

The mailman is appalled. He stands up, reaching for the government-issue pen tucked behind his ear.

Of course, this absolute untruth need not be what Otto implied. But something definitely went down, because right after I got the scribbled note the mailman started giving me dirty looks. Not that I really cared. What hurt most was Otto's betrayal, his going behind my back. After all we'd shared. Had he heard me on the phone making the appointment to get his nuts clipped when I brought him in for his shots in the fall? Was it my taste in dog chow? Whatever the case, Otto now had plans of his own. I had no choice but to put mine on hold while I went into reconnoiter mode.

The next night when I got home from the office, I showed Otto the written-on wrapper. He sniffed it then feigned indifference, acting submissive and loyal as usual, licking my hand, rolling onto his side. I played along and scratched his belly, but he wasn't fooling me. I'd noticed the teeth marks on the binoculars, and the fact that they weren't where I'd left them. I began to watch him more closely. He was spending a lot of his time outside, licking his chops as he paced the fence near my sunbathing neighbor.

The next month, my lovely neighbor brought over and shoved into my mailbox the July issue of *Juggs* that had seemingly been delivered to her house "by mistake." Through the front window I saw Otto with his big paws up on the fence, working his jaw, speaking, it looked like, though I couldn't hear anything over the air conditioner. She paused and scratched his head. I didn't need my binoculars to see his desire for her shapely leg. That bastard dog. That actor. I regretted ever telling him the specifics of my desire.

I waited until she was long gone before I went to get my magazine. There it was again, the same scribbled word, *Creep*. I considered the penmanship. The cursive was a bit loopy, but in the end I determined it was written in a decidedly masculine hand. How embarrassing for my neighbor to have seen it. I thought about reporting the mailman, but chose not to. I needed to focus on Otto.

When I called Otto inside that evening, I didn't scold. I set his bowl of dog chow on the table and added a few pieces of my steak. He took to my chair like it had been his all along.

"You've been so good lately," I said, "You deserve to spend more time inside enjoying the air conditioning. How would you like to start sleeping on the bed?"

Otto played dumb, wagging his tail as he licked his bowl clean, but he couldn't hide the thoughts behind those big browns: one day he'd just hop the fence and she'd be all his. Jealousy snarled through me. I decided the time had come for me to go with my instincts.

I put the Animal Channel on 24/7 and started filling a second water bowl with beer. I heaped Otto's plate with meat. I made sure he was within earshot when I called to cancel his appointment to get neutered. He put on a quick ten pounds and lost interest in the yard. Pretty soon he was sauntering around the house like it was his paw print on the mortgage. Meanwhile, I started spending most of my spare time outside, patrolling the perimeter, dealing with those overgrown hedges I wanted to dig out. Let him cool his heels, I figured. Give him a taste of the gilded cage. See what it reveals.

Sure enough, one of the first things to fall away was the mute routine, though I don't know if it was the beer that dropped his guard or if he just decided to dispense with the cover because he thought he was top dog. At first, I did find odd those talky, mewling growls he started making when I came into the house after a day of "working the lot," as I like to call it, but I've since gotten used to them. I have learned to pick up on his tone, how to tell if he's pleased or angry about something, though the specifics of what he's getting at remain beyond me. Which suits me fine, actually, because all the work in the yard has caused me to realize that talking is a waste of time. I rarely speak to anyone now, though I suppose I will have to call the office back eventually. Even the mailman has started to look at me in a new way, almost like he wants to give me a pat on the back. I figure it's because he can relate to someone who appreciates being outside. Even that advice my old man offered during my youth right before he ran off to chase a bus going God knows where finally had the chance to sink in. "Listen, son," he said, "Some say. Some do. You remember that."

But the best thing about taking the fight to the enemy (the enemy being my own failure to realize that this is and always has been a solo mission) is that I'm getting into great shape. My legs feel almost bionic, like I could tear around the yard for hours or take the chain-link fence in a single bound. All the digging has stripped my belly lean and put the hardness back into my arms. Even my sight and hearing and sense of smell seem to have improved, changes I attribute to the fresh air.

There are other things, too, things you wouldn't expect. Like who'd have ever thought a good roll in the dirt could be so damn refreshing. I also feel a whole new sense of ownership for this yard now that I've pissed on every tree on the lot. Of course, let's not forget the view: my neighbor has turned brown as a walnut; and, looking up from sweaty work, I've caught her smiling my way more than once lately.

Otto seems happy enough with his new situation, though sometimes I think he gets a little depressed. Just yesterday, I'm pretty sure I saw him moping at the bedroom window trying to figure out how to prop my binoculars on the sill. I buried the urge to feel for him and went on digging for those moles that have been tearing up my lawn. By the time I got inside, he was zoned out on the couch in front of some special about show dogs. He barely sniffed in my direction when I passed by, stinking of mole. Right then I knew he'd fully surrendered. Sunk so deep into creature comforts he'd lost his edge and pretty much resigned himself to letting the world pass him by as he watched my neighbor from afar.

From what I overheard her saying on her cell phone as she sunbathed today, my neighbor is planning to have a few friends over tonight for a backyard barbeque. I haven't checked, but I've got a gut feeling we're due for a full moon. This seems a perfect opportunity for us to get acquainted— without interference from Otto. I suppose the appropriate way to handle it would be to lean up against the fence and simply introduce myself, make some pleasant conversation, and hope she invites me over. But, as I mentioned, I've come to believe talk is a waste of time, so I'm considering doing something a bit more dramatic, like leaping over the fence into her yard with a bouquet of flowers or a raw porterhouse clenched between my teeth. Who knows, maybe once we've had our fill of meat and rose petals we'll decide to go running wild on the town. I might even think about Otto now and again while we're gone, if only briefly.

I imagine I'll come home elated just before dawn, reeking of a good romp. Otto will be waiting up, stewing in a mix of anger and heartsick worry. I suppose he'll have every right to be mad at me for taking off all night without letting him know where I'm going. He might even decide to give me the silent treatment, though I'm sure he'll have a lot to say once I tell him I was actually calling the time when I pretended to cancel his appointment for the old snip snip. But I won't care, because I'll have the girl. And he's welcome to the rest, everything inside, all the stuff and distraction meant to dull the purposelessness and empty longing that comes with being afraid to just go tearing after what you want. That's right. I'm taking the yard and the possibilities beyond.

Admittedly, my transformation has brought with it a certain amount of pain. Otto was supposed to be my sidekick, my in, and he betrayed me. Though I guess I should be grateful. If Otto hadn't forced me to rethink the plan, my neighbor would surely have rejected my pathetic former self, and I'd still be drunk and out of shape and sitting on the couch looking at the latest issue of *Juggs*. Besides, it's not like Otto hasn't gotten what he wanted, in a way. Air conditioning. The bed. A full refrigerator he can pull open by the dishtowel I've tied around the door handle. A few weeks after they snip him he'll feel nothing more than a vague sense that he's missing out on something in life and settle right back into his long naps and TV and beer. Who knows, he might even start putting pen to paper just to kill the time, looking for ways to explain his newfound discontents. How much more like a man could he ever hope to be?

## Arion Resigns

Mutiny is the last I remember. Being pitched over. Only to
awaken here. Drowning in an Aeron chair. Typing my own
ransom memo for the corporate pirates who pay me in
somnambulistic days. Unsure how I was fished out and tanked.
I fill an ironic window on the 22$^{nd}$ floor. The Fisher Building
scrapes dun sky above Detroit ghettos. Peregrine falcons give
shape to gnarled winds. Snatch pigeons from the currents. Only
to set gutted featherbones within reach. Upon my sill. I eat
years. Dolphins and humpback whales dive over and again
down the blue mural decay of the Broderick building beyond.
Eventually someone calls a meeting. In it I ask who drifted my
life away on hot sirens rising from the steaming streets. This is
what no one wants to talk about. Of course. Our talk is
deliverables. Project status. The milky muse of my brain sours.
Pours over mouthfuls of suspect words. Synergy. Milestone.
Benchmark. Bleeding edge. The omnipotent R.O.I. A burning
furrow worms my gut. Afraid of the sleep threatening to dream
me fathoms deeper. I sip my nth cup of black. Mull the word
*talk* until the sound turns crow: *Talk. Tawk. Cawk. Caw. Caw.*
Swim back to my desk against dead seas. Stalled by the very air
I've forgotten how to need. This is what's left. Facing the life
I've wrought. A comfortable near-miss namesake chair. A
window on the 22$^{nd}$ floor. My hole in space just beyond the

sill's rail leaking the dregs of a wine god's song. Painted, peeling dolphins wondering if I will leap. Or pick over these remnants. A pigeon carcass. The falcon found unworthy.

## The Death of a Henchman

He reads the letter on his bunk in the barracks after mail call. She's through waiting and is leaving him for that salesman with the nice car. His brothers in arms tell him to buck up—what's a woman except a shot to the heart that doesn't kill you but won't heal.

The alarm tries to ring itself off the wall. Hands peel rifles from the rack. Boots flash through the barracks doorway. There is much yelling and falling out: a Hero has breached the Evil Genius's compound.

His first glimpse of the Hero is from a distance. The Hero is a whirling, white-hot light his uniformed brothers in arms rush toward. He understands, finally: all this time the moth has been trying to extinguish not marry itself to the flame.

The Hero breaks the bodies of his brothers in arms. The Hero sends the broken bodies of his brothers in arms flying in brutally fantastic ways. *Fools*, he thinks of his broken brothers in arms for blindly rushing in—even as he rushes in after them.

# I Am and Always Will Be

*If you're losing your soul and you
know it, then you've still got a
soul left to lose.*

Charles Bukowski

She was the morbidly obese, middle-aged lady living in the downstairs apartment of the rental house we shared. "My appendix almost burst," she said by way of a greeting one day as I climbed the front porch stairs to find her hunkered down in a creaking lawn chair, the word *SUGAR* stretching in a sparkly silver distortion across the chest of her pink sweat suit. She pressed her hands lightly against the lower right side of her massive belly and exhaled jaggedly. "Got staples on my insides," she said. "Stitches, too."

We'd never talked much in the two years I'd lived there. In fact, I did everything I could to avoid her. It all just seemed too obvious: the garbage bags full of diet cola empties; the broken, second-hand toys her grubby, screaming grandkids left strewn across the dead lawn; the wet hackings of her obnoxious, cackling friends rising to my open windows on the smoke of their Virginia Slims.

Typically, I'd just offer some perfunctory greeting and go upstairs to my apartment and be done with her. But this day was different, by which I mean *I* was feeling different on this day—a sunny, fall afternoon of chirping birds and turned leaves rustling in the wind-stirred trees. The smell of grilled meat hanging in the air. It was a day so perfect it seemed fake. A good day to have off from the Jiffy Lube. A day that somehow allowed even a shitty street like ours to shine with the lie that all will eventually be right with the world. And that, along with her morbid greeting, had pulled me up short.

I'd only come home from the bar to grab my flask before heading over to the park to enjoy the golden evening I could feel coming on, but now, with the beer buzz and the turned leaves drifting down through the angled afternoon light, I found myself doing something I never would have done before. I asked how she felt.

She drew a deep, rattling breath, the SUGAR stretching further as she curled her lips back in a grimace. I saw myself slotting quarters between the gaps in her stained teeth while waiting for music to leak from her stitched abdomen. "I'm in some pain, but not too much," she said.

Quick as my feelings of good will came on, they faded. I'd already lost interest. Obviously, she was going to live, was fine, blah blah, all that shit. And I wanted my flask, my sunny day walk. I said I was glad she was okay and made a move for my apartment door. Then she reached into the pocket of her sweatpants and pulled out a bottle of painkillers. Rattled them.

"They gave me these," she said.

I eyed the bottle with envy. OxyContin. I told her those would do the trick. She nodded and set the bottle down next to her can of diet cola on the stained TV tray at her elbow.

"Hey," she said, "You got anything to read?"

Up in my apartment was a stack of tabloids I kept next to the crapper: *Bat Boy Escapes. Teenage Joy-riding Aliens. Titanic Survivor Speaks from Inside Waterbed. Woman Uses Glass Eye to Spy on Cheating Husband.* Just the kind of junk I thought she'd like. I told her sure I did and went upstairs to get them.

When I held them out, she shook her head. "Oh, no thanks, I don't read that stuff."

I shrugged, turned around, and dropped the tabloids into the yellow recycling bin at the porch's edge.

"Say," she said, "What's that book in your back pocket?"

She meant my beat to shit paperback copy of Shakespeare's *Julius Caesar*, a relic from my single year at community college, a prop I stared through so I wouldn't look stupid drinking in bars alone. Not a single woman, or man for that matter, had ever started a conversation with me by asking what I was reading, though I still continued to carry the book around. I'd read parts here and there, but the truth was I could care less about Shakespeare. I was usually looking over the top of it at the TV.

I pulled the book out. It had worn to the curve of my ass like a wallet. I handed it to her, told her it was a play; I didn't think she'd like it. She smiled, once again showing me the ruined pickets of her teeth.

"The fault, dear Brutus, is not in our stars but in ourselves," she said.

I had no idea what she was talking about. She read the confusion on my face.

"Sorry," she said. "The pills got me kinda loopy." She flipped through the book, found the page. Pointed out the line.

Through the windows of her apartment I could see a row of photos on the mantle. Among them, an old black and white of someone in an army uniform as well as a recent color shot of a young Marine, stiff and unsmiling in his dress blues. On her walls she'd taped up her grandkids' crayon scribbles of purple trees and green suns next to what looked like a few diplomas or certificates of some kind. I took it all in, the evidence of her love, her loyalty, her attempts at self improvement, and I had to stop myself from laughing out loud as it became abundantly clear to me that I am and always will be a totally self-absorbed, judgmental asshole. I wanted to slap her in the face. Punch her repeatedly in the wounded side for reminding me of this. Instead, I shook my last two smokes out of the pack, lit them together, handed one to her, and sat down on the stoop at her feet.

She was right. So were Shakespeare and Caesar. In the end, we decide. I tried to think of something to say about the play, which she'd obviously read and understood, unlike me. There was this line I'd come across once that had stuck with me for a while, but now I couldn't quite remember it. Something about butchers pardoning the bleeding earth for being meek and gentle. I groped for the sense of its meaning, felt some understanding there on the edge of my mind. Then what little I could realize slipped away as I decided to tell her how bad my back had been hurting me lately.

# Tagged

*Please God help me so that everyone*
*who passes by learns to love my Jesus.*

Billboard: US 131 North

I dropped the first tab around 5:00 p.m., walked up to the convenience store, bought a twelve-pack of PBR, then climbed the ladder of a freshly posted billboard edging the highway where I stretched out along the slim, metal ledge and waited for the acid to take hold. The rushed hours of Monday's commute home unscrolled below me, vibrating the iron, pushing a steady sigh of tires and the hum of so much displaced air up through the grating against my back. I had just quit my job at Jiffy Lube a few hours before because the manager had tried to force me in on my day off, so I said screw you and your strong-arm tactics. It was a warm spring evening coming on, and I wanted to wipe my soul clean of the grime so I could reassess my situation. I needed to remember what it was like to feel life surging up from the core.

SUV after SUV after SUV after SUV blew past below. The acid started breaking the world down, eating away the surface of reality, pulling back the veils. Each car became a blood cell coursing through a grey ribbon of vein. The vein became a strand in a phosphorescent web. The web became a net wrapped around a ball hurtling through a void. Every single molecule of the atmosphere, which I could see and stir with my hands, seemed charged with an innately obvious yet ultimately untranslatable meaning.

Sometime after dark the billboard floodlights snapped on to spotlight me at the trip's peak. My muscles ignited with the firings of an ancient, universal, electro-chemical reaction. Rolling over onto my stomach, I pushed myself to my feet in the warm night and stared up at the billboard, across which was smeared a gigantic, weeping child with her hands clasped in prayer. Her lips were moving. The writhing, now audible, words writ large above her head pulled me toward a vortex of absolute understanding; somewhere in the infinite spaces between what she was saying and what I was feeling there was an eternal testament on the spun dust of all matter. The only thing left for me to do was claw past what had been papered over to expose the truth.

I tore through that outer layer to discover a story with infinite endings, all of which I saw instantly and understood at once. In one conclusion, I rip and flail at the billboard's wrapping like a toddler mauls a birthday present, only to lose my balance and tumble from the ledge to my death. In another, it's the police bullhorn that finally brings me to, and after an incomprehensible screed punctuated by hurled beer cans, I am taken down with a tranquilizer dart to the neck, falling from on high into the fire department's safety net where I am hog-tied, tagged, and carried off for further examination and potential prosecution.

In the ending I decided to keep, I hear the wolfish wailing of their sirens and the low growling of their engines on the wind miles before they top the highway's rise. I smell the unnatural exhaust of their furious hurry, and without thinking I shed my oily human skin, swing down the metal trunk's rungs hand over hand, the meat and guts of me falling from glowing bones as I go. So that I touch the ground at last stripped of all but a naked, radar instinct that cuts me through the scrub lining the highway to the dark back streets where I know without thinking how to light my way home.

## Getting Beaten

You're just this side of Jackson, MI, speeding east on I-94, listening to the college football game on your Honda Civic's radio. It's a crisp, October Saturday afternoon of bright sun and clear blue sky. Oak and Maple, their leaves flaming yellow through blood-orange, line the highway, but you're not paying attention to the change of season. You aren't really even seeing the road. Driving on mental autopilot, watching the game unfold across the screen of your mind, you're starting to get very pissed off because things are not going well for your team.

"No! No! NO!" You slap your hand down on the dash at the interception, the violent arc of your arm spinning the cheap, 3D eyeball necklace that hangs from the rearview mirror. Shouldering back into your seat, you white-knuckle the steering wheel as the archrival's safety runs the interception back for a touchdown.

It is hard to believe how fast this game has turned. First, a blocked punt taken all the way back for a TD, and then this interception—all in the last few minutes before the half. A few miles ago State was up ten to seven. Now, as the extra point goes through, they're down to U of M twenty-one to ten. You take a pull off the hangover Gatorade and snort a disgusted laugh. On those few occasions when you actually care who wins a game, your team inevitably falls apart, even during a rare

113

season when they're heavily favored. It's as if there's some kind of cosmic jinx attached to your allegiance.

U of M kicks off, and you're already visualizing the fumbled return. Definitely snap the radio off then because, jinxed or not, your throbbing, whiskey-crippled head won't be able to take any more. State returns the kick to their own thirty-five with just under a minute to go. More than enough time for a hurry-up offense to take a few shots at the end zone or put them in range for a quick field goal and little momentum going into the half. Then the Spartan coach calls three fullback dives in a row and has the QB take a knee on 4$^{th}$ and 9 to run out clock. You drive along, gritting your teeth, the band's tinny brass ringing through your swollen brain.

It's your fault, this mood. Late and hung over, last night's fight with Cheryl, more than two hours' drive to Marlboro's house in Detroit where you're supposed to be watching this game with your buddies as a warm up to Donnie's bachelor party: all of it just bitter sauce on top of this debacle you shouldn't care so much about.

So what if it's the biggest college football rivalry in the state. So what if you spent four and half years wandering loaded around the campus and through the bars of East Lansing. So what if you fell madly in love, in the true sense of the word, with a woman while you were there, and the two of you proceeded to destroy your hope of a future together with cheating and drunken drama. So what. It's just a football game. You don't even have money down.

The Spartan band blares the fight song, and you flash on those home games with your college buddies. The Idiots, as you were known to others, screaming drunk in the stadium's student section, passing around the bottles of schnapps snuck in under coats. Eventually, someone a few rows below would grab a co-ed and hoist her up over everyone's heads, guys copping a feel as she was carried past screaming in delight or anger—no one cared which—hand over hand, above the crowd and tossed, for all you ever knew, over the lip of the stadium like a virgin thrown off a cliff as a sacrifice to the gods of Score.

You flip down the sun visor to block the glare knifing off the rear window of a late model Volvo diesel sedan going too slow in the passing lane, further annoyed with having forgotten your sunglasses. The right lane is wide open, but you still zoom to within feet of the Volvo's rear and highlight the *Keep Your Ideology off My Ovaries* and *Practice Random Acts of Kindness* bumper stickers with a flash of your brights.

The Volvo starts slowing down, sixty, fifty-five, fifty. You flash your brights again, tap the horn. You catch her eyes darting to the rearview. This passive-aggressive shit drives you nuts. You hit the turn signal and get ready to take her on the right when the Volvo starts to drift into the slow lane. "Moron," you label her as you stomp the accelerator down and pull even.

She's a youngish nouveau-hippie type: ratty white-girl dreads, nose ring, loose hand-knit sweater, probably alpaca or whatever. She looks early twenties, six or seven years younger than you, and she's cute. "What's your problem?" you mouth at her closed window. She's shaking her head righteously, refusing to even look at you. "Oh, yeah, that's it," you say, "I'm the one with the problem for wanting to drive the speed-limit and use the passing lane to pass people." Reaching angrily across the passenger seat, swerving a little as you do so, you crank the window down.

"Hey!" you yell at her rolled up window between glances at the road. You notice a pack of cars on the horizon. "Hey!" You honk the horn this time, and she finally glances over, a little fear showing on her face before she quickly looks away. "Love your mother," you shout, and you flash her a peace sign along with an ugly smile before hitting the gas and leaving her behind.

"Fuckin' bitch," you spit, surprised at your vehemence as soon as the words leave your mouth. You see the irony in your hassling a cute hippie chick: you, quite the hipster with your Caesar cut and goatee and white T-shirt beneath a biker's leather, a grotesque face custom painted by one of your many artist friends adorning its back. A few years ago it would have been a whole different scene if you'd spotted her from across the room during some show or reading or opening at State. You would have put the slick move all over her, bra-less little neo-hippie girl with soft hair covering her legs.

You were a Liberal Arts Major, Journalism Minor; you used to wear the uniform: long hair in a ponytail, paisley shirt, ripped jeans and Birks. You would have fingered your earring, put down the government, gone on about reality trips and poetry while you pumped her full of free wine or keg beer. You would have talked about karma and the cosmic soul and the synchronicities of a connected universe. Talked an endless river of confused, altruistic, ambiguous crap and meant every word as you swam her through the drunken crowd and off into a darker room.

Not anymore. These days your friends are all about wedding plans and navigating middle management. They're getting into 401Ks and looking to buy houses. Meanwhile, you're pushing thirty and still living hand to mouth with bad teeth and no health insurance, barely making bills and party money while working as a free-lance reporter for the arts and entertainment section of the *Midwest Gazette*. You've done your best to justify your lack of more traditional ambitions by convincing yourself that your friends' soul-stealing suburban lifestyle would kill you. But you see the plans they're making, the money they're saving, the families they're talking about starting, and you're beginning to wonder who the real sell-out is.

She can't drive worth a damn, but she's a cutie, that girl in the Volvo. The more you think about it, the more familiar she seems. If she's a little older than she looks, you might have talked to her at some bar or kegger. Easing up on the gas, you search the rearview. You could slow up and wait. Get another look at her to be sure. Maybe mouth an apology. But you're late and feeling poisoned from last night's booze. You have other things to worry about, like if you still have a girlfriend. You flick the glass and plastic "holographic" eye hanging down from the rear-view mirror on its fake gold chain, a piece of dime store crap. "So I can keep an eye on you," Cheryl had joked when she hung it from the mirror a few months ago. The eye swings back and forth as you drive, winding and unwinding itself.

You round the long curve that comes just before Parma and see the huge, neon sign for the Booby Trap lit up full blast, even though its mid-day. The strip bar sits on a rise at the side of the highway, and the red, flashing *Live!–Nude!–Girls!* catches your attention every time you take I- 94 to Detroit. Usually, seeing the sign makes you think about pulling off for a few quick beers and a face-full of cleavage. Today, the place makes you think about Cheryl and last night's fight.

The evening had started out well enough. Drinks and a little grilling out over at her apartment. She'd known about the bachelor party for weeks and didn't seem to mind that you were going. Until she brought it up as the two of you were clearing the table after the meal.

"You guys will probably have a pretty wild time tomorrow night, huh?" she said as she slipped the dinner plates into the sink. "Are they planning on having strippers or anything?"

You nodded and smiled, dumped the extra salad into a Tupperware bowl and snapped down the lid. You'd been expecting this all along and were surprised it hadn't come sooner.

"Yeah, maybe some dancers from a strip club. No big deal."

"Boys will be boys. I guess," she said.

And that was all, and you thought, *Damn, I'm getting off easy.*

A little while later, when the two of you were sitting on the couch, heating up, she asked you softly between kisses and unbuttonings what kind of things went on at your friend's bachelor parties, were there ever, "You know, prostitutes and stuff. I mean, it's fine, I trust you. I just want to know."

It was a legitimate question, if loaded and badly timed. Normally, you would have steered around it, lied and told her there was never anything more than a few topless dancers and some porno movies, but the question had somehow gotten under your skin. Obviously, it wasn't fine. Obviously, she did mind. And her asking while saying she trusted you was a sure sign that she didn't trust you at all. You'd cheated on all your long term girlfriends, but never her, at least not yet, though you didn't plan to, and so you came at her with the self righteous smarm of the guilty convert.

"You really want to know?" you said, leaning away, crossing your arms. "Or are you just hoping I'll lie so you can choose to either believe the lie or call me a liar?" And though you understood that you were destroying all your chances for the evening, or worse, you told her in graphic detail about the lesbian "toy show" your buddies had arranged for the last few bachelor parties you'd been to, and how you assumed they'd do the same for this one.

You had a good buzz on, and the sense of displacement you felt while giving her the details made it all the more surreal as you became the audience of your own destruction. Because even though you saw the change on Cheryl's face, you went on describing exactly what the girls did to each other. Then you drove it home by telling her how after the show the girls sometimes went off into another room with a box of cling wrap to give twenty-dollar blowjobs, and that a lot of the guys would go for it, though never you.

"What's your problem?" she asked once you finished, more venom in her voice than you'd ever heard, "Why do you have to be such an asshole?"

"Does that mean you would have preferred the lie over the truth?" you said.

She stood up and stared you down. "Unlike some people who are going to watch a "toy show" tomorrow, I have to get up early for work," she said. "You probably shouldn't drive. You can sleep on the couch if you want." And she left you there in the dark, bathed in the glow of the TV.

You sat for a while, thinking about going back to your own apartment then deciding not to. Maybe after she'd cooled off a little you could slip into bed with her, press yourself against her warm back, say you were sorry, tell her again that you weren't one of the ones who went with the girls. You grabbed the remote, cabled in on a wildlife show and sat there in the flickering light, feeling an odd mix of self-righteousness and self-loathing while you watched a warthog trample a snake. It was true: you'd never cheated on her and you didn't plan to. You could cling to that. You finished your drink, then hers, then made another and brought the pint back with you to the couch where you nipped straight from the bottle until it was empty.

She was already gone when you woke up late the next morning on the couch, shoes still on, not even a sympathetic blanket tossed over your legs. Head razed, you went into the kitchen and drank a few glasses of water before seeing the note she'd left on the table next to your car keys: *GROW UP* was all it said.

You wadded the note and left it there on the table, grabbed your keys and started to walk out. Then you thought better of it and went back and took the note and shoved it into your coat pocket. You stood there looking around her neat kitchen. According to her microwave, it wasn't even nine o'clock. You wouldn't need to be on the road until eleven to make kickoff over at Marlboro's. You opened the fridge and found a single beer. You took it down in a few long swallows then went to her bedroom where you pulled off your coat and shoes and got into her bed, smelling her on the pillows. Last night was fuzzy, but you remembered enough to suspect that her anger was something you had coming. Though you'd only been with her for a little over a year, this wasn't the first time you'd gotten drunk and said ugly things to her when she became even the least bit possessive. You thought about getting up to write an apology note, something equally simple and to the point like, *I'm sorry. I'll try,* but fell into an uneasy sleep instead.

You're still turning the fight with Cheryl around in your head when a sudden swell of cheering catches your ear as the teams run onto the field for the second half. You imagine The Idiots sprawled out all over Marlboro's living room: Donnie and Hankopolis and Fiasco and all the rest of them. They've got the big screen fired up, cases of beer, Spartan caps and sweatshirts on, a bottle of schnapps going around as they bitch about the way things are going with the game.

These are some of your best and oldest friends. You've been buddies with these guys since high school and then on into college where you lived like animals in a house in the student ghetto. You saw them almost every day for ten years, partied, hung out, road-tripped, all that wild youth bullshit. You even managed to keep it up for those first few years after graduation. Now, between everybody's jobs and moving and their serious girlfriends or wives, you're lucky if you can all get together once a month. Soon, the babies will start arriving, and that will be that. Everything's changing for your buddies, but you're still living in a dumpy apartment, going to the bar four nights a week, looking for something you just can't seem to name or find. You push the gas and take it up to eighty. Today is probably one of the last times you'll all be together for this game, and suddenly you're feeling very, very late.

You're chewing on the inside of your lip as the Spartans kick off to start the second half. "Jesus Christ, learn to goddamn tackle," you shout as Michigan takes the kick in their end zone and returns it past midfield. Then you notice you're doing almost twenty over and that your knuckles are white across the top of wheel. You back it down, check your rearview for cops. Any more points on your license and your insurance is going to be cancelled. Worse, there's probably still enough alcohol in your blood for a DUI.

___"Watch it, they're going long," you say under your breath, sitting perfectly still in the driver's seat, as if your focus on the down can actually make a difference in the Spartan defense's ability to perform.

Two plays later, Michigan passes for a touchdown and you snap off the radio in disgust. As far as you're concerned, it's all but over; the Spartan spine is broken, and you're not in the mood to put yourself through the ugly details of their complete collapse. Still, you can't help thinking all your superstitions will be maddeningly confirmed once you get to Marlboro's and find out you missed one of the greatest comebacks in Spartan history.

You lock in on seventy-six and drive in silence for some time, imagining what the party will be like tonight: the girls, the alcohol, the craziness. In your driver's trance, you approach and gradually begin to pass a tan mini-van on the right, a move that annoys you whenever someone else pulls it. You take a glance at the people inside: a balding middle-aged man, a plain, cross-looking, slightly chubby woman, a kid, a boy, maybe nine or ten, in the rear. You wince at the sight of them—this is your friends, maybe even you, in five or ten years.

The kid waves. *Nice kid*, you think. He puts his open mouth to the side window and does a blowfish against the glass. You point at him, grinning. *Funny kid.* Suddenly, as if all the rest were a set-up, the kid goes dead serious. He glances at his parents up front to make sure they aren't paying attention, which they aren't, because they appear to be arguing, and then he gives you the finger, really gives it to you with both hands, the double finger, putting his face into it, his nose scrunching, his front teeth clamping down on his bottom lip as he jams his hands up against the glass. *FUCK YOU*, he mouths. Fuck. You. It's disturbingly funny, funny enough to make you laugh out loud.

You're still smirking and shaking your head at the little bastard as you take a hand off of the wheel to give him the same right back. And you're in the middle of that smirk and offhand gesture when the woman in the front passenger seat looks painfully away from her argument just in time to see you flipping off her kid. Or her. Or all of them. She can't tell who, and she's giving you this disgusted and hurt look, as if your gesture is the icing on the cake of everything that has gone completely wrong with her life in a world of culpable men. It's the look of someone truly wounded, someone who's just endured a pointless, resonant cruelty, and as you meet those eyes you remember who the hippie girl you saw earlier reminds you of.

She must have been a freshman. She told you that night what she was, along with her name, but you can't remember either, of course. You remember only that it was your Junior year at State and that you and Donnie were walking back from the liquor store when you saw a few girls standing on the porch of a house party that was breaking up because the keg had run dry.

You stepped up, saw the long, dirty blonde hair, the naive look, the hippie skirt. "Party's just getting started at our place," you told her, holding up the half gallon of vodka. "Come on over." Then you and Donnie walked her and a friend back to your house.

You can't remember anything you talked about, but certainly you must have turned on the greasy charm, because after a few drinks and some grass, you peeled her off the couch, took her upstairs and, *Wow*, she said, the dorm rooms were so small; she'd never seen a room like this before: the best bedroom in that house, your water bed with silk sheets, your bad oil paintings on the wall, your guitar in the corner, your books and records and CDs all over the floor. You probably told her you were a painter, a poet, a musician, in a band, whatever you needed to tell her to make her think you were the artist she'd always wanted to get close to. You talked her into bed somehow, used some lie, some half-assed promise that implied your future interest, all the time knowing she'd be nothing but one night's lay. You remember trying to take her shirt off and that she wouldn't let you and that you didn't understand why until you slipped your hands underneath and felt the unbelievable Braille of acne that mapped her back. You'd never before touched a girl with skin like that, and it grossed you out, but not so bad as to make you stop. You must have said something perfectly calculated in that pause, the pause she always dreaded with a boy—"Doesn't matter, I still think you're beautiful." And maybe even partially meant it as you worked at her and worked at her with your hands, gently but ceaselessly, trying everything to get her hotter, begging, finally, like a high school boy begs, until she gave in, letting you slip her panties past her skinny freshman legs.

It was over before she even had a chance to enjoy it, and right away the first thing you'd wanted was to go back downstairs to meet The Idiots for a drink. You could feel the stereo pushing Mötley Crüe and Guns 'n' Roses and AC/DC up through the floor of your room. You could hear your friends shouting, but guilt kept you there in bed with her for just a few minutes longer as she stroked your chest, the same guilt that caused you to give her your real phone number when you drove her back to the dorm later that night. But you weren't too worried about it. You figured your friends could deflect her later if it came to that.

She started calling the very next day, and The Idiots played her off and played her off like you asked—until they told you she was starting to sound desperate, and you became afraid. Afraid she might somehow be pregnant, even though you'd worn a rubber. Afraid she'd say you date-raped her, which, if not literally true, was probably true emotionally. Finally, you got so worried you called her back, figured out she wasn't pregnant, said you were sorry you hadn't returned her calls. You hadn't gotten the messages. You'd been busy with classes. You didn't mean to hurt her but you'd gotten back together with your old girlfriend (actually, you'd never broken up and the whole scene had been a cheat on your part), and you were really sorry about all this and hoped you could still be friends.

For a while, you kept looking over your shoulder, expecting cops at the door. For a while you tried to hate yourself, swore you'd never do anything so vile and selfish again. For a while. Then you forgot about her. Done was done; it wasn't like you'd actually held her down and physically forced her to do anything. She hadn't said *no* or *stop*. And what were you supposed to do after the fact anyhow? Turn yourself in? Hurt her more by starting a relationship with a girl you didn't care about that would only end badly?

Stepping on the gas, you leave the mini-van shrinking in your rearview mirror. You turn the radio back on, immediately dial away from the game and look for some decent tunes. But the image of girl's face and the memory of the feel of her acne-covered back against your hands will not fade. The mid-afternoon sun drills down from the sky, putting a wicked glare into the rear window of the cars ahead. What you did to that girl; what you're doing to Cheryl; what is wrong with you: all three are too ugly to think about. A wave of pain curls over your ears and into your temples. You grab the Gatorade and suck out the dregs as a Burger King billboard shoots by. "HUNGRY? 15 miles," it reads. You think you should get something on your stomach if you're going to start drinking again so soon.

You're pushing buttons in the passing lane, still looking for a station, trying to keep yourself distracted when you see the high-beams flashing in your rearview: a black pick-up doing at least ninety, bearing down. You check the speedometer. You're going eighty-three, thirteen over. To the right, the center lane is wide open, and there are no other cars in sight. You check the rearview again. The truck is still coming on, lights flashing a rhythm, the faces behind the windshield emerging now—a couple guys in baseball caps. Screw 'em, you decide. They can go around. But the truck keeps coming, closing fast, the flashing quickening, then the high-beams staying on as the pick-up's grill fills the entire rear view mirror of your little economy car. You just shake your head and keep your eyes locked on the road. They can go around.

The impact against your bumper almost causes you to lose control of the car. Adrenal heat races up your neck and back, burns along your arms. You can't believe someone has actually rammed you on the highway. The audacity of it is almost too much to believe. "Motherfucker," you scream into the rearview mirror, and you can see the stupid, satisfied smiles plastered across the faces of the two young guys in the cab before the grill fills your mirror again and you quickly pull into the right lane.

You crank down your window, the thunder of wind filling your ears and whipping your hair as the truck begins to pass. "What the fuck is wrong with you, man," you shout. The passenger in aviator shades and TKE hat gives you a bored look and somehow manages to toss a half-smoked cigarette through your open window. "You're bumming, dude," the guy shouts as they pull away. You catch a glimpse of the flag attached to the truck's doorjamb—a golden M on a dark blue background. You step on the gas, pushing the little economy car to eighty, ninety, ninety-five. You know you're risking a huge ticket, the loss of your license, but you don't care. No one can pull that kind of shit on you and get away with it. Asshole frat boys. That was crazy what they did. What if you'd been some old lady or someone who couldn't keep control of the car? They could have killed somebody. You. That family in the mini-van. That hippie girl in the Volvo. What they did. It was just wrong.

You pull up tight next to the passenger side of the truck and whip the empty plastic Gatorade bottle at the door. The wind sweeps the bottle away the instant it leaves your hand. The frat boy passenger in shades looks down. "Pull that fucking truck over right now," you shout. The guy gives you a blank look then leans out of your line of vision. The truck swerves suddenly toward you, and you jerk the wheel to avoid a collision, then jerk it back again to avoid the tight shoulder. You cut in behind the truck, making stupid passes to stay in pursuit. You're imagining a pistol into your glove box, the way you'd wave it in smoker-boy's horrified face before pumping a few bullets into the bed and engine. Suddenly there is the red flash of taillights, and you brake hard, almost losing it again, but remembering to turn into the slight skid. They keep tapping the brakes, trying to get you to back off or wreck your front end on the wide chrome bumper. They don't care if you hit them and trash your car; they don't care if you hit them and go through the windshield and snap your goddamn neck. Your heart is pounding. The truck's driver hits the gas, the powerful engine growling. You're about to speed up and go after them when you have a vision of exactly where this is headed: you nearly bursting the Honda's engine to pull ahead and cut them off, your car and the truck tangling into a spinning wad of twisted metal rolling down the road. You ease off the gas and let them go. Only then do you realize you should have at least had the sense to get their license plate first. You pound a fist down on the dash. "FUCK. God fucking dammit." That's when you remember the lit cigarette floating around somewhere in your car.

A few miles later you see the Burger King sign on its pole high above the expressway and decide to pull off to get some food and check out the damage to the car's rear bumper. You're still worked up, but at least you've stopped swearing out loud to yourself and pounding the dashboard of your car, though you can't shake that queasy, broken feeling of being violated.

You're about to pull into the Burger King when you notice the frat-boys' pick up parked at the Mobil station next door. Something tells you to just let it go, but you know you at least have to pull in and get the plate number. Donnie's older brother is a private investigator. Get the plate number and you might be able to find out the driver's address. Once you have that you have all kinds of options. Wait a few weeks to avoid suspicion and you and the Idiots could make a weekend raid to sugar his gas tank, break off toothpicks in his door locks, tie a dead squirrel underneath his truck. Maybe even follow him home from a bar and jump him—show him what it means to have someone hit you out of nowhere.

The truck's cab is empty when you pull in. You park in the space next to it and see through the station's glass doors that they're up at the counter with beer and chips. The passenger notices you staring and elbows the one who must be the driver. You keep a hateful stare on them as you get out the car and slam the edge of your door into the side of the brand new truck. The driver's face tightens with rage. You lean into the door, hearing the edge grate along the truck's front quarter panel before you close it. You're standing behind your car, looking at the good-sized crack in your plastic bumper molding when the driver comes outside and drops his twelve-pack of cans down hard on your hood.

"Like what's your fucking problem, bro?" he says, throwing out his hands.

You walk quickly toward him and get right up into his face. He doesn't even look old enough to buy the beer he's just thrown down. He's a little taller than you are, and wiry, but you're pretty sure you can take him.

"My problem?!" Your hands dart out, twisting up the front of his flannel as you drive him back and slam him into the wide window of the gas station, cracking the glass. "You're the one with the fucking problem now," you say. "You almost drove me off the road back there! I'm putting you under citizen's arrest for reckless driving." You ball the driver's shirt up under his chin, start leaning into him. The cracked glass grinds.

"I didn't do shit, dude," the driver says, his hands finding your wrists and pulling.

"Shut up!" you say, "Just shut the fuck up. I'm taking you inside and we're gonna call the cops and settle this, or I'll kick your fucking ass right here and now."

"Try it, man," and you turn your head slightly at the words just in time to catch the passenger's sucker punch on the side of your mouth.

Still holding onto the driver, you reel back, dragging him along as you fall through a stacked display of washer solvent to the oily cement. He's on top now, puddles of bright blue liquid foaming around the two of you as you thrash. You bring a knee into his gut and leg the driver off then sit up to see two mechanics in stained coveralls coming on, long wrenches at the ready. You've scrambled to your feet and are lurching after the passenger who has just reached the truck's door when you feel the mechanics' hands take hold.

"Let go of me, goddammitt!" you scream, bloody spit flying.

The driver, also back on his feet now, sees his chance. He steps in and punches two quick shots into your face before you can get your arms free to protect yourself.

"Hey. Hey!" one of the mechanics says, but the driver has already turned away. He kicks the Civic's front quarter panel hard with a heavy boot, leaving a black smear.

"I said let me go!" Jerking yourself loose from the mechanics, you feel a muscle in your shoulder tear. You take a few shaky steps toward the truck, but it's too late, the driver is already behind the wheel and turning the engine over, pulling out fast. He's reached the street by the time your vision clears.

You face off with the mechanics. "Why didn't you grab him, too?!"

"You just cool down," one mechanic says, "fight's over."

"Unless you want more," the other mechanic says, pointing you out with the wrench.

"You have no idea what's going on," you say.

"You owe me for a window is what's going on." It's the manager standing in the door of the Quick Stop, a robust, leathery woman with long blonde hair. "And don't you try driving off like those two did neither. I got your license number."

"Did you get theirs?" you yell, taking a step toward her as the mechanics put themselves between you. "Tell me you at least got theirs."

"Didn't see as I needed to," the manager says. "Pulling up here and nailing their truck like that with your door. Looked to me like you started it."

You're parked at the other side of the Mobil's parking lot, staring at the ticket in your hand and thinking about tearing it up. Before leaving, the cops told you they weren't going to take you in because they still needed to sort some things out, but make no mistake this kind of public disturbance is misdemeanor, if not a potential felony, and you'll be getting a notice to appear for arraignment in the mail. As for what had happened on the expressway, since you don't have a plate number or any witnesses, there isn't much they can do. You gave them the color and the make of the truck, descriptions of the driver and passenger. They said they'll try to keep an eye. Maybe you've got a case if they find a witness or can locate the vehicle and find some of your car's paint on its front end.

The manager approaches your car. She reaches in with a surprisingly muscular arm and drops a Mobil business card in your lap. Trina Sole: Manager.

"The police gave me your phone number and address," she says. "I'll call when I get a price on the window. It'll probably cost you around five hundred dollars."

You ignore her.

She gives a little huff of disgust. "Yeah, I see how you are," she says and walks away.

After she leaves, you turn on the radio and try to get the game. It's Wisconsin against Iowa now. You can't help snorting a laugh and wondering if the Spartans found a way out of that mess once you stopped rooting for them.

You check yourself out in the rearview. One side of your lower lip is cut and fattening. A circle of bruised blood is beginning to bloom beneath your left eye. You wonder if you should just screw the bachelor party and go home, apologize to Cheryl. She's a better woman than you deserve, probably the best one you'll ever find. Maybe she'll forget her anger and mother you once she sees you've been sucker-punched and you tell her why.

But you'd never hear the end of it if you missed Donnie's bachelor party. Never. And maybe you should just forget Cheryl on general principle for being so over-possessive and go to that party and get a twenty-dollar cling wrap blowjob from a stripper you'll never see again. Maybe you've had enough of being tied down to a girlfriend. You could sell all your stuff, buy a motorcycle and a pawnshop pistol and ride off with a wad of cash in your pocket. Live on the road. Whatever. That girlfriend you failed with at State is out there somewhere, Oregon last you heard. Enough time has passed. Maybe you could look her up. There is a whole world of things a single man can do. Only how come it all seems to feel like a dead end?

You reach over and take a beer from the twelve-pack the frat boy left behind. At least the manager overlooked that much. You pop the top, slurping up the foam as it tries to wash over the edge of the can. The beer stings the cut in your lip, but you take a good swig anyway before setting the can into the cup holder. Back in your second and third years of college, right around the time you did what you did to that freshman girl, you used to drive around the sticks outside of Lansing with the Idiots, drinking beer. You can still see the sun of those years falling through the trees, the steady bars of light and shadow beating over the road. There was always music too loud on the radio, always a bottle going around, always big talk about who was getting laid and how often. Back then you were all driving nowhere because nowhere was exactly where you wanted to go. Windows rolled down, the inside of the car busy with wind. You were young with your future ahead of you. What's your excuse now?

You reach inside your jacket pocket and feel a crumpled piece of paper: Cheryl's note. You un-wad it and stare at it, then crumple it up again and shove it into the ashtray. You turn over the engine, put the car into gear and pull back onto the access road to the expressway. It nearly makes you physically sick to think of those two driving on to whatever party they're headed towards, cranking their tunes, slapping high-fives over how they got the best of you. You can imagine how they'll change the story when they tell their buddies about "totally kicking this dude's ass." You look down at your hands. They're shaking, but you're not sure if it's from rage or shame over that helpless feeling of being held defenseless while the driver punched you in the face. It isn't right, your being left to bear the brunt, your being fined, your having to pay for the window while they just drive away. What kind of people were they? How could they think they could just do whatever they wanted to somebody and get away with it? People needed to pay more attention to consequences.

Reaching the intersection, the point where you have to choose what happens next, you can feel it doesn't matter any more if you go west or east, back home or to the party. As long as you're going nowhere in the larger sense, nothing's going to change.

You pull over to the shoulder, take another good look at yourself in the rearview mirror, your fat lip, the cheek below your eye starting to swell the eye closed. You fish the note out of the ashtray, un-crumple it and watch the words go blurry as you tear up. Is this what you've become, or maybe what you've always been, a stunted soul, someone who puts himself ahead of everybody else? It's not so long before the answer arrives, dripping from your slobbery lips in two words. But you'd have to take yet another step back to even hear what's being said. You'd have to imagine yourself a few hours ago, before a fight you were smart enough to avoid, seeing someone like you parked on the shoulder of the access road as you headed back toward the highway with a full tank of gas and a bag of hamburgers on the passenger seat. You'd have to pull to a stop next to this someone and take it all in: the poor, beaten up bastard parked there, crying and mumbling. You'd have to be ready to ask him if he's okay, if he needed anything. You'd have to want to help in the first place before you could roll down your window to hear him saying over and over, "I'm sorry. I'm sorry. I'm sorry."

# Accepting Inner Change at the Grocery Store

You're in the grocery store checkout line minding your own when the man behind you barks out, "Fuck you." At first, you're not sure who he's talking to, so you turn around, right into the shock of seeing yourself arrived in your own future, twenty-odd years added to your face, greasy food smeared into the snarls of your gone to seed beard.

"Fuck you," he breathes again across those teeth you keep forgetting to floss, and the stink of it says you're exactly the one he means as he stares the words into your eyes.

"Yeah, you. Fuck. You."

Shirking work, already listing with a five-beer buzz, all you want to do is get back to your girlfriend's and send barbeque smoke up into the gloaming. You're not ready for this ragged doppelganger standing in line behind you with no purchase in his hands.

You try to parse it out in your scattered, shot-through brain. Who sent this nut to whip your ego with a vision of the future escaped from the black hole in your head? Who put you, twenty years down the road, up to calling you out from your unknown Then for the past lapses of your addled Now? And what, exactly, did you do to deserve being fuck you'd in a grocery store by a vision of your ne'er do well time-traveled self? Step on your own foot? Look at yourself wrong in your own mind's eye? You have no idea, but deep inside you intuit— no—you *believe*, you deserve the hard seed at the heart of this.

Staring at what you surely can become, sizing up such a very real and ugly threat, you subconsciously hedge your bets and think, of all things, *There go I but for the grace of God,* a conundrum of self-determination you've heard the devout mouth after the unfortunate. Then your present tense comes roaring back. *Man, you look like fucking shit, dude,* and the mirrored point in that shard of truth sheds its light upon your life of indolence and self-indulgence in a way that makes you promise for the millionth time to start getting better. Tomorrow.

"Fuck you," he says a final time for reasons of your own, this ragged wanderer painted in Dorian grays.

"Exactly," you say. And you turn your back on him, giving your attention to the increasingly nervous cashier, thumbing out bills for your beer, your pint, your onion, your lettuce, your pound of ground beef, before accepting the change she lays across your palm, gathering what you've paid for, and moving on.

# III

# GHOST LIMBS

*Then there are those human-shaped*
*patches of crystallization*
*on the stone bridges of Nagasaki*

John Woods, "Owning a Shadow"


*All the rest of our lives*
*the tree outside that window*
*groans in the wind.*

Philip Levine, "February 14"

## Bad Juju, 1989

"Just do what you want. That's what you're going to do anyhow," Peg says as she looks away from Hal, out the passenger window at green Missouri rushing by. She notices her ghost in the glass, her tired eyes, and wishes she and Hal could just quit all this bickering and be happy. Once, they were the kind of lovers who would have spent the last two hundred miles holding hands, massaging napes, talking about all the things they'd do once they got to New Orleans. Now they cover the distance arguing.

She stares at the road ahead, the green-scummed drainage ditch stretching away from them like a clogged artery, and she thinks about how different this Hal is from the Hal she used to know. The funny Hal, the considerate Hal. She wants that Hal back.

All the way down from Chicago they've fought about more things than she can keep track of, just now finishing what she swears is the last argument she's going to let herself be drawn into—this one about, of all ridiculous things, the voodoo queen Marie Laveau and her tomb off the French Quarter in St. Louis Cemetery Number One. So much pointless jockeying over who's right. All this dissection of who said what and exactly what they meant. Things have gotten so she isn't even sure who the two of them are anymore. Lovers. Roommates. A couple beginning to turn their backs on each other.

"I knew you'd say that." Hal slaps his palm against the wheel. "I knew it. I shoulda ripped that page out when I first saw it. Guided tours are lame, Peg. I'm telling you, you're afraid for no real reason. Just like always. Like it's gonna be bad juju or something."

Hal shakes his head in disgust, then reaches out and turns up the tape deck too loud. Coltrane squeals a bleeding line of high notes. Peg resists the urge to snap the music off.

Bad juju. What's he trying to do, pretend he's a local or something? Like he knows anything about that stuff. Why can't he just admit there's nothing wrong with following good advice? "St. Louis Cemetery No. 1 is dangerous. Don't go there unless you're with a guided tour during the day." There it is in black and white in the AAA Tourbook, for God's sake. It doesn't matter if he thinks there's nothing to worry about as long as they're careful. When does she get to be right, after they've been mugged or she's been raped? What's she supposed to think when it seems his being right is more important to him than her safety?

Up ahead she sees a sign for a rest stop. "I have to go to the bathroom." She almost has to shout it above the music. She can see the muscles in his jaw clench as he nods. So it's come to this, she realizes. She can't even tell him she has to go to the bathroom without pissing him off.

An endless line of pines blurs past. These days it's as if everything they say is loaded, as if turning up the car radio or suggesting they take a tour has to mean something beyond what it normally means. They can't even have sex anymore without her feeling like he's trying to prove something. Two years ago he asked her to move in with him, a move he said would help prepare them for marriage. Two years later and they're not even engaged, and with the way things have been going lately she's not sure she would even say yes to the proposal she knows isn't coming. She can't tell exactly when or how this plaque began to form inside their hearts, but as far as she's concerned, this trip is a last chance to try and save things.

Hal lays a gentle hand on her thigh, strokes her leg through her jeans. This bothers her at first. She considers pushing his hand away, but knows that would only start the two of them off again.

"I'm sorry," he says. "Really. Please. Let's not argue."

She puts her hand on top of his and sighs. She always caves. They'd been friends for over a year before they finally got together. The night they first kissed by the bonfire at that party, she'd pulled away long enough to say, "It's about time." And it was true, she had waited for him, holding back her secret desire all the way through the ugly crash and aftermath of his last relationship. She wants to work this out, to believe they're still in love, but she's had enough of his stubborn need to be right and all the stupid, childish risks he likes to take. Almost thirty and he's still sneaking liquor into movie theaters, trespassing through fenced-off fields because he wants to show her a frog pond or some abandoned building he's found, breaking into his old middle school at three in the morning to steal the cow skull he remembered sketching in the sixth grade. It's not that she's against taking risks or that she doesn't like to have a good time, but the decisions she sees as growing up and growing into the rest of life, he just chalks up to the flaws he's pinned on her character, her weakness and fear.

They take a sweeping curve and the brilliant sun, low on the horizon, pounds her eyes. Up ahead, a little murder of crows peck at a heap of mangled flesh on the highway's shoulder. The birds rise on the displaced air as their car breezes by. It's a doe carcass, legs splayed wide, the head bent impossibly backwards toward the tail.

Hal watches Peg drive through the night, her tired face luminescent green in the glow of the dashboard. He has his seat leaned all the way back, his hands clasped across his stomach like a corpse. It's his turn to get some sleep, but rain thuds a metallic rhythm on the roof of the car, and beneath his feet he can feel the tires' wet hissing as he rolls the word *hydroplaning* over and over in his mind.

Just past Grenada, Mississippi, before the rain and right after Peg started driving, they saw the wreckage of a horrible accident and the body. They'd hit the scene before police or paramedics. At first, Hal thought the slowing traffic merging to the right shoulder and the waving flashlight in the near distance were not for an accident at all, but for one of those roadside checkpoints to search for drugs or drunk drivers. Then he noticed in the flickering light of the road flares that the flashlight waver was a paunchy, middle-aged man in dress pants and a button down shirt.

After he'd waved them slowly past, they saw a few cars pulled against the median wall, flashers on, their headlights making something solid out of the growing fog. Then came the wreck: a pick-up on its side in the middle of the four lane highway, the bed and cab accordioned from the truck's rolling end over end. Beyond the truck, in the near distance, a few people stood helplessly around the body which, thrown clear, lay wrong in a twisted heap on a slash of centerline. The stop and start of cars eventually brought them parallel to the corpse, and Hal saw that the man lay uncovered, his arms flung out as if giving something up. Blood, black and reflecting the headlights, had pooled around his obscenely dented head. Then the car jerked to a stop, throwing him forward into the dashboard.

"What the fuck, Peg," he said, blinking into the red brake lights of the Blazer they'd almost rear-ended, "Can't you keep your eyes on the road?"

"Give me a break," she said.

This bitterness in her voice was something he'd been hearing more and more of lately. Frankly, her shitty attitude was starting to get on his nerves.

"Don't look," he told her. "You don't want to see this."

Peg shook her head, rolled her window down. "Is there any way we can help?" she asked a man standing apart from the others.

"No," he said quietly. "Just keep driving, please."

"Tell them they should cover the body," Hal said, but Peg ignored him, rolling up her window as she locked her eyes on the Blazer's brake lights.

Soon the line began to move again, the bottleneck gradually widening, cars spreading across the lanes as they pushed their way back to speed. Hal twisted around in his seat to have a last look at the wreck as it shrank away behind them. He found it hard to believe they could see death so closely then leave it behind so quickly, back on their way to something as trivial as a vacation. A few miles later, the hard rain started.

Now the fat drops fall so fast and thick the wipers on high barely throw the sheets of water aside. Hal knows he needs rest if he's going to drive through those bleak hours that will come just before dawn, but since the wreck he's been too worried about their own accident to sleep. Peg's driving has always made him nervous, and the heavy rain has him feeling every tentative pass or slight swerve she makes. He listens to her swearing under her breath at the wet thundering of a high-balling semi that slaps their car unsteady with sheets of water as it passes. He puts his foot down on the phantom brake and thinks about asking her to pull over so he can drive. But he's been driving since they left this morning. She needs to carry some of the weight if they're going to road-trip straight through. He imagines briefly the mangled horror of their own accident, sees the twisted wreck of their car from above as if disembodied, and Peg crying, standing next to an ambulance throwing arcs of siren light against the rain as a paramedic finishes pulling up the zipper on a body bag.

Hal thinks of Marie Laveau and what a stupid thing she was to fight about. It's not like he actually believes that stuff about putting your mark on her tomb to get your wish. But ever since they'd decided to take this trip he's been reading up on voodoo. Reading about people like Marie Laveau and the Chicken Man, datura plants, and the blowfish poison used to turn living people into zombie slaves in Haiti.

He finds it all interesting enough, but he realizes he has only a callow, white man's understanding of the religion. He does feel some kinship, though; he's kept a makeshift altar in every apartment he's lived in since college, long before he'd ever read anything about voodoo. It's little more than an eclectic souvenir stand, but he's still nostalgic and superstitious enough to believe each object arranged there has a power tied to the positive energy of some experience or person or place in his life. Every now and then, when he's missing someone or thinking of his past or hoping for something to come out a certain way, he'll light a cone of incense and the Virgin Mary of Guadalupe candle and the Sacred Heart of Jesus candle then sit before the statuettes, animal bones, shells and stones to focus his thoughts.

The only reason he even wanted to go to Marie Laveau's tomb in the first place was because he'd heard the cemeteries in

New Orleans with their fading mausoleums were something you wanted to see. But Peg's saying no without checking it out first, saying no without even really knowing what she was talking about, just going blindly by some guidebook's warning—it was exactly the type of thing that was annoying him.

Peg puts the Grateful Dead on the radio, probably to help her relax, but she knows he can't stand that band. Between her driving and the music how does she expect him to get any sleep? He levers his seat upright and puts on his glasses.

"Any good dreams?" Peg asks him.

"I wasn't sleeping."

"You were snoring."

"You're the one who snores."

Peg shrugs and nudges up the volume. "Right. Of course I am."

The song ends and the crowd starts cheering. He wonders if she was at that show. Before they'd met she once spent a whole summer following the Dead in a van full of her friends. He's seen the pictures of her in the print skirts and tie-dyes, close-ups of that big smile, those swimming, dilated pupils where he couldn't see the fear of anything. But that was before they moved in together, before she cut her ass length hair to her shoulders for that new job at the Women's Shelter, before she started harping on him about getting married and quitting the music store and using his college degree to get a "real" job. She wasn't like that at all when they first started dating; she seemed to be a seeker like him. She seemed free, and he can't help but wonder if she'd have given him so much grief over the tomb if she knew about the engagement ring in his backpack.

He has everything planned. Before hitting the Jazz Festival, they're driving to the end of Louisiana's Highway 1 to camp a few days at the state park on Grand Isle. And that's all she thinks they'll be doing there. But after they've set up the tent and slept off the long ride, he'll take her for a walk on the beach. Looking for shells, he'll bend down as if he's found a good one. "Oh, my God!" or "Holy shit, look at this!" he'll say and hold the ring up to the sunlight so it shines. Then he'll take her left hand and slide on the ring, which he's had sized to fit perfectly. "I can't believe this," he'll say, "Looks like we have to get married now," and he'll get down on one knee right there on the beach and swear he means it.

Once she says yes he'll tell her the whole thing was a lover's scheme, but for the moment he wants her to believe that their engagement was sealed by fate or a chance they'd then have to shape with their future.

Peg looks over at him, taking her eyes away from the road for what he feels is too long, and he resists the urge to tell her to pay attention to her driving.

"I'm getting tired," she says, "I've pretty much driven this whole tank, you think you can drive soon?"

Hal lets out a sigh. Can't she tell he's tired, too? He's driven two and a half tanks to her one, and she knows how hard it is for him to sleep when she's driving. She's already caught a few hours of sleep, he's had none, and now she'll be out and snoring ten minutes after he's taken the wheel.

"Forget it if that's the way you're going to be about it," she's saying when suddenly the road narrows sharply into a chute of flashing yellow lights and cement median walls. The traffic heading north, separated from them before by a wide stand of trees, is suddenly right next to them, semis blowing past, headlights burning. The car shudders over a pocked section of asphalt, and Hal's afraid Peg's about to lose control. He instinctively goes for the wheel then stops himself and turns down the radio instead.

"Get off at the next exit," he tells her, reaching into the darkness at his feet to feel for his shoes.

Peg and Hal wander through the French Quarter crowd, go-cups in their hands. They pass the open door of a strip club on Bourbon Street, and Peg notices a beautiful if trashy-looking woman leaning against the entrance in a tiny halter top and pair of sequined microshorts. The woman catches Peg's stare, flips up her top and lets her breasts spill out, "Laissez les bons temps rouler," she says, her voice deep as a man's. Peg looks away. Only to find Hal ogling.

"Wee wee" he says to Peg, laughing, elbowing her idiotically like she was his beer buddy.

A mounted cop clomps by. Hal holds up his plastic cup of whiskey as if to toast him. The cop watches Hal slam the drink and toss the cup down among the rest of the litter in the street. The cop shakes his head but keeps on riding. Hal pulls his forearm across his wet lips. "Ahhhh," he says, "I love this fucking town."

Peg hates it when he gets this way, dragging her from bar to bar, up and down the streets, acting like he's twenty one and just let loose on the world. It's gotten old. But this time is different, and she's worried. She couldn't believe it when he pulled a diamond engagement ring out of the sand the other morning. But how was she supposed to know it was something he bought, not something he'd actually just found? As if she'd want to wear some poor woman's lost ring for the rest of her life, maybe even a drowned or murdered woman's ring at that.

She could still see the hurt and confusion on his face as he tried to explain. It was the first time in a long time where he'd done something thoughtful for her, buying a ring, planning ahead, and he had to go and goof it up with some stupid idea about the marriage of chance and fate. A year ago she probably would have said yes once she understood, but now there's this ugly part of him she'd never really seen before. The way they've been getting along lately, especially these last few weeks, she isn't sure she'd have said yes to him even if he'd asked her in the normal way. She still loves him—and she told him so over and over while she struggled to keep up with him on his stiff walk back to the campground—but a wedding would only be a distraction from the things they still need to work out. She tried to make clear as gently as she could that she wants their wedding to be something other than a bandage, but he wouldn't listen.

Hal points a finger past her head. "Let's go there," he says, "I need another drink."

In the open doorway of Jean Laffite's Peg can see the dark, candle-lit tables, the ceiling lined with wooden beams. It could be such a romantic place, she thinks, if only. Hal heads directly to the counter and waits for a bartender. Peg hears what sounds like a live piano coming from somewhere. She walks around the corner and there it is, like she's only seen in the movies, a piano bar surrounded by people on stools. She walks over and takes a stool, pulls another near her for Hal.

The piano player, a handsome, older black man in a sharp suit, splashes a few delicate chords as if in greeting. She smiles at him, takes a cigarette out of her purse and lights up. He gives her a friendly wink and a nod.

Hal walks up with a Jim Beam on the rocks and a bottle of dark beer. He sits down heavily on the stool next to hers.

"Thought you might like to try this," he says, sliding the bottle of Blackened Voodoo toward her, "They brew it here in town."

"You know I don't like dark beer," she says.

"Okay," he says, "I'll drink it then."

They sit at the piano listening to the music in silence until a waitress comes by. Peg orders a Lemon Drop and a Dixie beer. She's tried to be fair with him, tried to be honest, but he won't listen. She didn't say she didn't want to marry him ever, just not right now. Getting married won't solve anything. He knows that, but he's too freaked out over being rejected and the fact that she might actually be right to admit it.

The waitress brings the drinks and Peg catches Hal checking out her ass as she walks away. It's nothing new, just one more thing about him that she dislikes but has tried to accept. She doesn't think he's ever cheated on her, though she wonders sometimes.

"Cemetery's only a couple blocks away, you know."

"Don't start, Hal."

"We should go check it out," Hal says. "We could make a wish together." He finishes off his whiskey, chases it with a big swallow of beer then belches into his fist. He grins an ugly grin, "We could wish you loved me enough to marry me."

"That's a mean thing to say."

"It was a mean thing you said to me on the beach."

"There's nothing mean about being honest."

The song ends, scattered applause, then Hal's voice too loud in the silence after, "You've got us divorced before we've even had a chance to try."

The piano player splashes a few notes and breaks the silence by saying something about welcome to the Big Easy as he starts into the next song.

Hal gives her a stare she can't read, a look somewhere between pity and disgust. He makes a show of slamming his beer, setting the empty bottle down loudly on the piano.

He takes forty bucks out of his wallet and drops it next to her cigarettes. "I'm going," he says, "I'll be back in an hour."

"I won't be here," Peg says without looking at him.

He stands there, staring at her, considering. "Your choice," he says, and he walks off, bumping his way through the crowded bar.

Hal threads the crowd down Bourbon Street. He steps into a doorway near the intersection of Bourbon and Bienville and pulls out the tourist map he got from the receptionist at the hotel—exactly the kind of thing he can't stand being seen using—and figures out the way to St. Louis Cemetery #1. He shoves the map back into his pocket and moves on. After a few blocks he's left the noise and lights behind and the streets are dark and empty. He's lost her. She can say we need more time to work things out or whatever else she wants, but her no means it's over. Why else would she say it? She's the one always bringing up marriage.

Get ourselves straightened out. What was that even supposed to mean? If he's overly critical it's only because he loves her and wants to stop her constant second-guessing and worrying from killing the flow of a good time.

He doesn't know what his next move should be. When he tries to see into their future, it's blank after a certain point, and what little he can see isn't that appealing: they'll probably offer each other half-assed apologies tomorrow, finish out the vacation, maybe even live together for little while longer, but it's clear now that she'll come to him one day soon enough to say she's leaving, and by the time he sees the cemetery a few blocks ahead he's wondering if it wouldn't be better for them both if he just ended things before they get any worse.

Hal steps through the open cemetery gates and sees the mausoleums glowing bone-white beneath a nearly full moon. From what he's read, Marie Laveau's tomb is next to the main path and impossible to miss, covered the way it is with the scratched Xs of tourists and believers. Thinking it will be easy enough to find, he walks off into the maze of tombs. Soon, the gate is lost behind him, and he can't decide if he's gone too far or hasn't gone far enough. He considers turning around and finding his way back to Peg and the bar, but the idea that that's what she would want him to do causes him to press on.

When he finally turns a corner and finds the tomb, small and scratched all over with Xs, the sadness of their situation wells up inside him. The last thing he needed was for them to fall apart. He's tired of trying to find a woman who fits, and he just doesn't think he has the energy to start over again with someone else. But all that explaining Peg tried to do on the beach, her talk about how he's changed, how critical and selfish he's become—it sounded just like what his last girlfriend said when she broke up with him, and he resented having to listen to that kind of shit a second time.

Hal walks to Laveau's tomb and touches the cold concrete, runs his finger over a few of the marks scratched onto its surface. Inches from his hand a crack stitches its way along the tomb. Out of the crack grows a scraggly vine. He snaps off a spindly branch and sticks it in his pocket—another souvenir for his altar. Suddenly he remembers the legend about Laveau's granting wishes and snorts a laugh, trying to think of what to wish for. It doesn't matter. He knows it's not for real, and even if it was he doesn't know the prayers or whatever else you probably needed to know to make it work. Even so, after all that's happened, making the right wish seems important somehow.

Going through his pockets, feeling for something to etch his mark with, his fingers touch the car keys, then the small, velvet ring box he's carrying around just to spite them both. For a second he considers using the diamond to make his mark. He imagines the sound of the diamond scratching against the stone, then decides against it and pulls out his car keys. He holds the ignition key ready like he is about to unlock the door, but he still has no idea what he wants to wish for, and he knows he'll never be able to decide.

Thinking vaguely that he just wants the whole mess resolved, he scratches his X onto the tomb.

As he turns to walk away, he hears a shoe scrape against the grit of the walkway right behind him. He looks back in time to see the blur of pipe coming down against the side of his head. He drops to his knees, arms loose, his keys jangling against the cement as he keels over onto the ground. He hears the keys being taken up then feels fingers in his pockets, first pulling the ring box then his wallet with their hotel key card out of his jeans. He tries to say something; he wants to sit up, but feels himself being sucked down into unconsciousness. The last sound he hears before passing out is the sharp little creak of the ring box opening followed by quiet laughter.

When Hal comes to, he is alone. Confused, he pushes himself up, wondering at first what's happened. Have they had a car accident? Where's Peg? Then he remembers. How long has he been here? What if that son of a bitch figures out what room they're in? He might already be back at the hotel waiting for Peg. And the guy has the keys to their car, their apartment back in Chicago, even the back door to the music store. He has Hal's wallet with his license, his address in it. There's no telling what could happen now. Hal staggers up and leans against Marie Laveau's tomb while he tries to get a hold of the spinning world. The goose egg on his head accelerates its throbbing.

He touches it gingerly, feeling it squish beneath his fingers before he pulls his hand away. No blood—at least there's that going for him.

She was right, he thinks. He should have listened. To the pounding in his head he puts together what's been the matter between them: he's guilty of judging her according to who he thinks she should be instead of simply loving her for who she is. He retches, starts to slide down the wall of the tomb toward the ground as a sickly, warm weight pours over him. He wants to sleep, just for a little while.

It's the fear of what could happen next and the hope that he may not be too late that gets him up and staggering back along the path toward the entrance. When he finally reaches the gate, his throbbing head forces him to stop. He's thinking about the ring and how he still owes two thousand dollars on it when fireworks start going off in the near distance. At first, he isn't sure if he's imagining them or not. But they keep exploding as he stands there trying to steady himself, one hand against his head, the other clinging to a gate he wishes had been locked in the first place.

More than an hour has passed and Hal is not back. Peg leans against the piano top, chin resting on her palm, empty shot glass at her elbow. Commander Willie Robadeaux, as he has introduced himself to the room, has been playing anything anyone calls out, mostly old jazz standards she's never heard of, but she still thinks they're wonderful.

"When the Saints Come Marching In" someone yells. Peg sees Commander Willie grimace slightly then fall an octave in the song he's playing before slipping into some weird, modal version of the tune. "That's not how it goes," the voice says. "Play it the regular way." But this time Willie cuts him off with a run of dissonant chords before rolling on. Peg sits up, catches Willie's glance, smiles at him.

"No, leave it just how it is," she says, "it sounds good sad like that." Commander Willie nods. He is a handsome man, she thinks. Forty, maybe forty-five, a little silver in his tight, curly black hair. She's never heard anyone play the piano like this, drinking and telling jokes and showing off and jumping from song to song the whole time. It seems like he knows every song ever written. Maybe later she'll throw him a curve and request a Dead tune like "Fire on the Mountain" or "Darkstar."

She checks her watch again. Hal should've been back long ago. Why did he have to be such a stubborn ass? Always right. Always pushing things, thinking only of himself. "Everybody dreams alone," he liked to tell her. What a bunch of shit. People in love dream together. Isn't that what love is?

He wasn't this way when they first started dating. He wasn't so reckless or judgmental or condescending. Or maybe he was. The longer this goes on the harder it is for her to remember what their life was like when things were good between them.

Peg pulls her last cigarette out of the pack and lights it. She takes a deep drag, jets the smoke out her nose. Nothing short of a big mistake will make Hal change. In her mind she sees him beat up or robbed and left for dead in some piss alley. She isn't sure if she'll be able to forgive herself if something horrible happens to him. She saw a TV show once about the vampires in this town. People who actually kidnap tourists and street people and keep them locked away in some back room so they can tap their blood and torture them. If that's for real, who knows what else is out there?

Her eyes get watery as she thinks of what she could have done to make him stay. If only she would have told him yes on the beach, everything would be different. Maybe she should have played horny tonight and asked him to take her back to their hotel room; maybe he'd needed more than words from her to show that she still cares. And she does care, for the Hal she used to know, not this person he's turned into. Maybe she should go find a cop.

She shakes her head against these thoughts then violently stubs out her cigarette in the ashtray. Screw him for making her feel this way. He's probably stumbling drunk in some bar right down the street. There's nothing she could have done. Hal does what he wants when he wants to, and if she says she doesn't like it, he shrugs and tells her he's never kept her from doing anything because she does that well enough for herself.

After Commander Willie finishes his set he picks up his drink and walks around the piano to Peg.

"How you, darlin?'" he asks, "Can I get you something?"

"No. No thanks," she says, but she's smiling.

"Hey, now. This is 'Nawlins. Lemon drop, right?"

Peg is surprised he's noticed. "Yeah, lemon drop. Okay. Sure. Thanks." She starts looking in her purse for her cigarettes then sees the empty, crumpled pack next to the ashtray on top of the piano. She turns to Willie, who's flagging the waitress. "I need to go get smokes," she says, "I'll be right back."

Peg is pressing the Camel Lights button on the cigarette machine and thinking she's been smoking way more than usual lately when she feels a sharp little shock in her fingertips like the machine is shorting out. Suddenly, a head-rush rolls over her and she feels a dizziness rising inside. She grabs the pack from the slot and hurries through the double doors to the patio for some air. She stands there, alone, looking through the wrought iron gate, gathering herself. She leans against the wall and watches the drunks howl and stagger down Bourbon Street. A couple, college-aged, passes near the gate. They're both slurring. Wasted. "I just don't wanna go in there is all," she says. "That's cool. Whatever you want," he says as he slings a drunken arm across her shoulders. Peg shakes her head and works on opening her pack of cigarettes.

Two smokes later Peg is about to go back inside when there is a huge explosion, and the sky erupts in splinters of green, then yellow, then blue light. She feels like she's falling, or more like the world is being sucked up around her, and she's afraid she's having a flashback, something she's never had before. Quickly as it came, the feeling passes, and she realizes the explosions are only fireworks over the river, probably for the jazz festival, which begins tomorrow. She takes a few deep breaths.

"Alright?" Peg turns to see Commander Willie. "Saw you wobblin'."

"I'm fine," she says, "Just needed a little air is all."

"You the boss." He hands her the shot and a Dixie beer, raises his glass, "To a lovely lady," he says.

"Laissez les bons temps rouler," Peg says, surprising herself with her memory of the stripper's French.

"Now you gettin' there," Willie says. They clink glasses, down the shots as another volley of fireworks explodes, lighting their upturned faces with shifting colors.

"First time they done this for the festival," he says.

"I've always loved fireworks," Peg tells him.

A muscular, young, white man with a waxed handlebar moustache and his short hair slicked and parted down the middle pokes his head out the patio doors. "Yup. It's fireworks," he drawls to someone inside, and Peg thinks of old-time bare-knuckle fighters—bare-chested gentleman in striped pants who could break a nose with one punch—as he comes onto the patio to join them.

Soon the small patio is crowded with people drinking and making a joke of oohing and ahhing, their faces tilted up toward the sky. Peg feels Willie pushed against her backside in the crush and she doesn't try to move away.

After the fireworks most everyone goes back inside, but Peg and Willie stay on the patio talking. Peg knows she is drunker than she should be. She leans up against the brick wall and listens to the hum of the quarter, the people, the music, a distant siren. When she shakes another smoke out of her pack, Willie is there with his lighter. Peg cups her hand around his, feels his skin warmer than the warm night. She looks at his face highlighted in the glow of the flame and wonders what it would be like to have sex with an older man, with a black man. Such a good musician. Probably has perfect timing, she thinks, and laughs.

"Finally in the mood to party," Willie says, "Alright. No good seeing a pretty woman so sad." He takes a brown cigarette out of a case he pulls from his suit coat pocket and fires it up. The sweet, heavy smell of cloves fills the air. "You feel like doin' something besides waiting on that grouchy man you come in with, you let me know. Lots a house parties here in the quarter if you want to get away from all this tourist stuff."

"Sounds like fun," she says.

"I get through this last set and we'll talk about it."

As he turns to walk into the bar, Peg grabs him by the hand and pulls him back to her, kisses him quickly on the mouth.

"Thank you," she says.

"Okay then. See you on the other side."

After Commander Willie is gone Peg sits down at one of the wrought iron patio tables. Her heart is beating quickly, and she can feel the tingle of adrenaline sobering her. Flirting is fine, but she never expected to surrender to the impulse of kissing a stranger, and she hadn't expected to like it. Hal is right about that much, she thinks, people should do what they want when they want to, as long as they're honest about it and nobody gets hurt. Nobody gets hurt. Maybe that's part he hasn't figured out yet.

She feels a burning in her stomach. Where is he? Should she call the hotel? Maybe she should just go back to the room and wait for him. She checks her watch; he's almost an hour and a half late. She decides to wait another fifteen minutes before calling the room and then maybe the police, though she knows he'll never let her live that down if it turns out nothing's wrong.

Peg stands, walks over to the patio gate and looks through, up and down Bourbon: neon pulsing everywhere, people staggering arm in arm, laughing, upending their plastic cups in the middle of the trashed street like it's the last party in the history of world.

Some vacation. She clenches her jaw, grips the bars. The whole city is bombed and she's getting an ulcer over a selfish little boy. Then, as if summoned by her anger, she sees Hal turning the corner onto Bourbon. At first she's so relieved she wants to scream his name and run after him. Until she notices how he's shuffling his feet, listing with a hand against his head, wandering like a goddamn drunken zombie back toward their hotel. Jesus Christ, she thinks, he must have stopped at every bar between Laffite's and the cemetery. Well, she certainly doesn't owe it to him to go back to the room to watch him puke. She'll deal with him later, whenever she gets back. Maybe she will go with Willie to check out a few of those parties. Or maybe she'll just stay out bar-hopping by herself for a while. Drunk as he looks, Hal is the last person she wants to be with right now. He may not think so, but she knows how to handle herself. She's been with plenty of men before him, had plenty of crazy times. Dropped more acid than he's ever seen. She was just sensible enough to let all that foolishness go and get on with the more important things, like trying to make some kind of real life for herself, or for the both of them, she used to think. But this is her vacation, too, and if this is the way he wants to play it, she can show him a few things about what it means to get wild. Let him worry about where she is for a while, if he's even awake to worry at all.

Piano riffs roll onto the patio through the open windows of the bar. Commander Willie is starting his last set with a torch song. "Darn that dream I dream each night, you say you love me and you hold me tight, but when I awake you're out of sight, darn that dream."

Peg feels the music wrap itself around her and lets go of the gate. She watches Hal shuffling along until he's swallowed by the crowd. He'll sleep like a dead man, she tells herself as she turns away. He'll never miss me.

## The Braid

Although Alex is thoroughly enchanted by Sondra's melodious voice and athletic figure and extroverted personality, what has truly stricken him is her long, golden blonde hair, the tremendously thick Nordic braid of it hanging well past her waist. And because of this, it can never be anything as simple as love at first sight when they meet during the company picnic at the state park that sunny summer day.

Alex and Sondra are two of this world's beautiful people. They are mid-twenties, flawless in their faces and bodies. Well-educated, from well-to-do families, they lead charmed lives. No sad backstories here. Just the nearly perfect now extending toward the promising future.

Sondra is on the verge of finishing her master's degree in Veterinary Science at the University of Michigan, schooling her parents easily, almost off-handedly, paid for. She's single and has come to this picnic with her girlfriend Marissa who works for the corporation where Alex, also single, is rapidly storming up the ranks as a CAD engineer.

Marissa is not surprised to see the subtext of attraction in their faces when she introduces these two to each other. She quickly makes an excuse about needing to keep her boyfriend over there by the beer cooler out of trouble and disappears.

Finally alone, Alex and Sondra sit at a picnic table and make small talk over barbequed chicken and potato salad. They're laughing at an anecdote he's shared about Marissa, how the morning after his promotion she snuck into his office and scotch taped every single thing to his desk.

"I didn't know that was *you* she did that to," Sondra lies. She's starting to really like this polite, handsome Alex, feeling her stomach knot a little each time he glances at her when he thinks she isn't looking, but she needs to pick his brain, see what's in his head. She stands her fork up in her potato salad and sets her paper plate on the picnic table.

"Do you believe God is the center of the universe?" she asks, because that's the kind of person she is, an agnostic who likes to throw people off balance.

"More like over to the side," Alex says.

"What do you mean?"

"Consciousness is the irony of mortality," he says, "You can thank God for that." "Oh, my. A perfectly ambiguous answer," she says, "Will you marry me?"

Of course she's only joking, but a little bomb goes off in his gut anyway. She's someone who knows how to throw a good curve. He admires that. And she's beautiful, besides.

"Would you like to go out to dinner with me next Friday?" he asks.

"And he knows how to be direct," Sondra says, "Yes. I'd love to."

"How about sushi. You like sushi?"

"Yeah, sushi's great," she says, "Nothing like nature in the raw."

Sondra stands up and stretches.

Alex takes in her figure, her tan legs, her shorts and t-shirt not too tight but showing off her firm shape, and he thinks she'd look damn good sunning on the foredeck of that speedboat he's going to buy with his promotion bonus. Then his eyes fall again upon her long braid, which swings before him now like a golden rope she wants him to climb. Sondra notices he's looking, and she smiles.

"I'm going to get another beer," she says, "You want one?"

And that's when George, one of Alex's fellow engineers, rolls up to the picnic area's parking lot with two All Terrain Vehicles strapped to the trailer he's pulling behind his brand-new Land Rover. Alex parties with George when they go to South Haven to work with the engineers at Whirlpool. Armed with nice suits, corporate expense accounts and their own hotel rooms, they've had their fair share of success picking up women in the beachside bars.

Sondra is the one who suggests they take the ATVs for a spin. She's driven them plenty of times before on her parents' spread. The daughter of a wealthy, hands-on horse breeder, she grew up shoveling manure, learning how to make herself useful, and living the cliché of riding magnificent horses through idyllic pastures with sunlight glancing off the waving, silken curtain of her golden hair.

Bouncing along on one of the ATVs, Alex follows Sondra down the trail. Having grown up in the suburbs of Detroit, he's only driven one a few times before, so he's taking it easy. The last thing he wants is to get dumped and end up looking like an ass. He likes being behind her anyhow, watching her rise up and down as she rides, looking at the braid she's coiled up against the back of her head and thinking of how he'd love to unwind it, sink his fingers into all that long, soft, blonde hair.

Sondra is pushing it a bit, showing off, when she bounces down into and out of a ditch that pulls her forward then leans her way back. Shaken loose by the impact, the braid comes unfurled and swings over her shoulder to her front side where it is snatched up in the motor. The motor whines hot as the braid is sucked into the gears and belts, instantly ripping Sondra from the seat, tearing off her hair at the scalp as the vehicle rolls on, pitches over, and stalls. She feels only as if she's been hurled down with incredible force then a sharp slicing into black unconsciousness.

It's the most fantastically horrifying thing he's ever witnessed, the only truly terrible accident he's ever seen. He leaps from his ATV and is at her side, t-shirt off to wrap her exposed, bloody skull. They are still in sight of the picnic tables, and the others have begun to notice something's gone wrong. "Call 911," he screams, but already more than one person has a cell phone in hand.

Alex realizes then that the doctors might want the scalp in an attempt to re-attach it as they do sometimes with fingers or limbs. Setting her head down gently on his blood- soaked shirt, he runs over to the ATV tipped on its side in the ditch at the edge of the trail. There is the dusty scalp dripping blood, pulled tight against the engine, the mangled braid coiled within. He finds a tool-kit under the ATV's seat and takes out a short, serrated blade. Gagging, he cuts the scalp free of the braid and hurries with it back to where she is stretched out in the dirt, still unconscious and surrounded now by people. Marissa is there beside her, holding Sondra's hand and crying.

When the ambulance comes he gives the paramedics the scalp, which they rinse in a sterile solution and put in a cooler. As he watches them carry Sondra back up the trail on a stretcher and put her into an ambulance at the trailhead, he tells himself that she will live, and makes a promise to be there to see her through all of what will follow.

The ambulance pulls away, red lights winking, the driver first chirping the siren in blips and fits then wailing it full blast once he's lipped the front wheels up from the gravel and is speeding out of the asphalt parking lot. Alex stands with the others, watching the ambulance until it's out of sight then listening to the fading siren.

The sobered up boyfriend leads a sobbing Marissa to her car. George stands in the middle of the parking lot talking on his cell phone to his lawyer—he can't get sued for this, can he? The shocked people wander back to the picnic ground to gather up their picnic. Instead of following them Alex goes back to the trail where he finds the ATV Sondra was riding, rights it, and slowly works what's left of the braid free. Would she want it for some reason? Should he keep it? Destroy it? What kind of life is this where people have to even consider such horrible, ridiculous things?

He turns away from the ATV, the length of oily hair clutched in his fist. Be there for her. Who is he kidding? All he could ever be to either of them now is the line between before and after, a reminder that everything comes apart eventually, if only to become something else.

He looks down at the mangled braid, considers the substantial heft of it, the countless golden hairs weaving inward upon themselves again and again. He touches the tip of its length, pulls off the elastic hair tie binding the end. Stands there, mindless, unwinding, getting oil-stains on his hands.

## No Retreat

Dad crunches down, bites a half moon into his toast, and I know it's his grinding teeth, and the greasy butter smell, and the little blob of strawberry jelly on his walrus-hairy lip that makes my bloated tummy cramp again. I huff a sigh and push my untouched cereal bowl away, check the time on the watch he gave me last month for my fourteenth birthday. A watch. Like I need a watch. Like I haven't spent enough time already staring at the stupid clock since I started school at Refuge, waiting on three, waiting to get the hell away from those nuns and priests and out of that uniform skirt and into Ron's pool. No. I need a watch. I need to carry every second I'm missing around on my wrist like some kind of punishment, even on a Saturday. I need to see the hands swinging exactly from seven twenty-nine and fifty-nine seconds into seven-thirty so they can remind me I've only got ten more minutes to talk my way out of going on this stupid loser retreat.

"I don't feel good," I say.

"Don't start," Dad says after he swallows and wipes his mouth on a paper towel. "You're going."

"But I got cramps," I tell him, and I hunch down into the kitchen chair and cross my arms over my stomach.

Dad wads the paper towel, drops it onto his plate. He leans forward, thumps an elbow down on the table, puts his big hand to his forehead and starts rubbing his temples with his thumb and middle finger. This is the way he likes to show me he's "had about enough."

Finally, he stops rubbing, pulls his hand away and stares at me. "You were at your mother's all week. Didn't she talk to you about this?"

"I told her you wouldn't understand," I say. But that's only half the truth. The other half is that she told me I shouldn't expect him to. And she did talk to me, though it's not like I'm going to tell him what she said about how some girls just get their first period a little later. How she tried to joke with me about my first "monthly" or the arrival of "Aunt Flo" or "being at the end of the sentence" or any of the other things she said about this bleeding I'm right on the edge of. He doesn't need to know how she made me walk around with that freaky Maxi Pad in my underwear for a whole day just so I could get used to the feel. Feels like a diaper is what it feels like, so I had to go get all embarrassed yesterday buying Kotex Thins at the drugstore. How am I supposed to tell him any of that when he's staring at me like I'm from another planet?

"Jesus," I mumble.

His eyes go hard. "You pick up that kind of talk from your mother?"

"Since when have you ever cared if I swear?"

"I know you didn't learn it at school."

Learn it at school. God. If he only knew what I was learning at school. Seniors in the bathroom giggling about how to give a good blowjob. Bragging about losing their virginity and actually looking forward to "shark week" and "Bloody Mary" showing up to end their worries. It's pathetic. The public school kids get the rep for being wild, but anybody with a brain knows the deal. Maybe the Catholic school freshmen are innocent, but by the time they graduate they're some of the loosest girls in town.

"They say Jesus a million times a day at that place. I wouldn't be saying it so much if I was going to Lakeview."

I see the jaw muscles beneath his stubbly cheeks bulge. This is getting on his nerves, but so what, I'm right.

"Since when do you even care about Jesus anyhow," I say. "You haven't gone to church once since the divorce."

"That's enough, Rachel."

"All summer my friends were talking about being freshman together at Lakeview, and I just had to stand there and listen. It's my life. I should be able to go to public school if I want."

My throat gets tight at the thought of everything I'm missing, and suddenly I want to cry, but I know crying only makes him madder, so I hold it in, turn the feeling into something angry instead.

"It's not fair," I say.

He sees I'm getting mad, and now he's being all calm on purpose, just to make me look stupid.

"You can do what you want when you're eighteen," he says, "Until then it's up to your mother and me to ... "

"But, Mom said ... "

"No, no. You're not playing both ends off the middle. Your mother and I agree. Refuge is a better school. We pay a lot for you to go there. You'll thank us when you get into a good college. Trust me."

"Let me go to Lakeview and I'll get all As, I swear. If I don't you can send me back to Refuge."

"C'mon, Rachel. I said that's enough."

"I hate it there. The girls are stuck-up and the nuns are mean."

"You've only been there a couple months. Give it some time."

"I have," And now I hate him because I can't keep myself from crying.

He's shaking his head as he gets up and goes to rinse his plate in the sink. The water hisses on, shuts off, he cups a few drips in his hand and wipes down his mustache. "I'm sorry." he says on his way out of the kitchen.

"Yeah, sure. Whatever," I say to his back.

Sorry. God, I can't stand it when he tries to make it sound like this is for my own good, like it's something I should be grateful for. I know the truth. I know why they sent me to that stupid school. To keep me away from Ron, his pool, his basement where his mother almost caught us before we could get our hands out from inside the front of each other's damp bathing suits. The real point is to put the nuns on me, keep my head full of too much homework and sad, perfect Jesus. This is about making sure I'm not a hassle for my parents who couldn't even manage to stay in love. Like they're the ones who should be telling me what to do in the first place. They don't know anything about anything.

The birdfeeder right outside our kitchen window is covered with noisy cardinals. Their bright red feathers flash in the morning sunlight while they hop and flap and crack seeds with their beaks. One seems to notice me and freeze. I can almost see myself in his shiny-black eye before he decides he doesn't care about me anymore and flies away.

Stupid Jupiter is still hot enough in late October that I'm sweating before we even reach the car. Jupiter, Florida. I might as well live on Jupiter, Jupiter now that I'm going to Refuge. I try to open my door, but it's locked, and then I get another cramp, and I remember shoving the brand new box of Kotex Thins into my backpack. For a second I just want it to start so the waiting can be over with, then I imagine what it would be like to canoe down a river with a pad moving around in my shorts and blood sneaking down my leg. "Oh, my god, she's leaking," I can already hear one of those idiot girls making fun of me. Nice way to start a rep as a loser. Maybe if I'm lucky it won't happen until I come back on Sunday.

"Quit with the attitude, Rachel," Dad says as he unlocks the car and tosses my sleeping bag in the back seat. "You like canoeing, at least you did when we used to go."

I slump down into the passenger seat and snap on my seatbelt. "I'm not a little girl anymore, Dad."

He puts the key in the ignition and starts the car. "No, you're not. And you're not going to have the same friends your whole life, either."

"All the friends I need are going to Lakeview," I say as I look out my window.

We take the side streets to Refuge. On the radio they're talking about the Berlin Wall coming down and Dad is shaking his head. "Everything's changing," he says.

The cramps start hitting me on and off and I remember the naked, pregnant women from my dream. They were standing in a long row with their bellies sticking out, more of them than I could ever count, in a white room that never ends, and each one had a little green ball floating just above her outstretched palm. They were all smiling at me as I walked past. I remember touching their big melon bellies. It was totally weird, but it was still kind of nice, actually, and I woke up feeling like somebody had just told me they loved me, until the ugly Refuge uniform thrown over the back of my chair made me remember what day it was.

We drive past Laurie's street. She's probably sleeping in—just like I'd be doing if I was going to Lakeview like I should be.

Last night, when I was complaining to her on the phone, she told me everybody says it isn't the same without me around. But at least we still have the weekends, except for this one, and after school. Sure. She's the one sitting in classes with Ron, talking to him at lunch, seeing him in the hallways. I wanted to slam the receiver down and pop her ear for being such a sneaky bitch. But I didn't. She'd just say I'm crazy. She'd say we're still best friends like always, even while she knows this is the perfect chance for her to get in the way of what I'd hoped for me and Ron.

I want to climb out of my skin when I think about how she'll spend all day today in her skanky little bikini swimming in Ron's parent's pool with the rest of my friends. Between her and all the other girls trying to get his attention, why should Ron even bother to think of me, stuck on the Our Lady of Refuge Fall Freshman Retreat, paddling down some river with a bunch of girls I barely even know. He never asked me to "go" with him. He never said kissing or touching me meant something like going together was guaranteed to happen between us. But Laurie should know better, and what about Tommy or Alex or any of Ron's other buddies who will be there too. God. Who am I kidding? I'll be in some stinky everglades when she hangs her legs over the side of the raft. She'll be the one laughing this time, hoping for the feel of Ron's hand, first around her ankle, then higher on her thigh as she's pulled under.

It's super-hot inside the school bus. I don't feel like talking to anyone, and none of them have ever really made much effort to talk to me, so I walk fast down the stuffy aisle and pick a seat near the back. I set my backpack and sleeping bag next to me to fill up the rest of the seat and pull down my window. Right below it someone's written "I want out" and "Eat Me" in black magic marker. It's the first time I smile all day. I wish I knew the girl who wrote it. I think about digging out a pen and adding "Refuse Refuge" or "Jonesing for Jesus" or something stupid or funny like that. Instead I just close my eyes and wish I had the power to speed up time.

When the bus doors close and we start moving and Father Kessel stands up at the front to talk about Refuge traditions and this "day of reflection," or whatever, blah, blah, blah, I realize I'm actually going to end up with a seat of my own. We pull out of the Refuge parking lot, a hot breeze filling up the bus, and Jupiter goes past in a shimmer of heat, like the whole city is stuck in the middle of melting. Everyone is talking, and I try to tune out their giggly bullshit about teachers and bands and boys they like or hate. "I hear Father Kessel never gives out A's in Freshman Theology...I totally love 'Like a Prayer,' that video is so awesome...He tried to get to second base, but I just pushed his hand away." Second base? Who even talks like that anymore? Stupid little girls who went to Catholic grade school together, Jesus and everything safe shoved up inside their heads. They don't know anything about guys or music. I'm probably the only one on this bus who's ever heard of the Misfits or the Dead Kennedys or the Ramones or the Sex Pistols or any of those other bands on that mix tape I borrowed from Ron. Ron. Drinking pop all day, belly flops onto the rubber raft from off the diving board. Water volleyball. Maybe pairing up when his mom goes out to the store. Second base. God, how lame. And their nervous laughing about it. They have no idea what it means to be touched where it counts by someone you like. I laughed into his mouth when he touched me between the legs with his cold hand that first time. My hand on his chest, pressed against his heart beating so fast, like he'd been running after me for miles. He laughed quietly right along with me, our kiss curving up into a smile as he pressed himself closer, eyes closing, dark spot growing warm between us, rubbing, electric skin. Which is the way I want to remember it as I let the engine's humming take their pointless voices away.

I wake up as the bus is passing through the park gate, slipping beneath a roof of trees into the green shadows where the air becomes wet like soaked sheets but doesn't get cool. Limbs slap the metal sides and drag along. A little scream and more giggling when a branch shoves a wad of leaves through an open window.

We jerk to a stop at the canoe livery parking lot and Father Kessel tells us to file off the bus, he's already picked our partners for the canoe trip. I'm glad we don't have to find a partner on our own. At least this won't be like standing around in the cafeteria looking for someone to sit with before I decide to just go outside and eat my sack lunch alone under a tree in the grotto.

We wait as Father Kessel reads our names off a list. Tan shorts and sweat stained T-shirt, white legs and skinny arms and limp grey hair poking out from under a fishing hat— without his rope belt and robe, he reminds me of some kind of tour guide. It's surprising to see him like that. I'd never imagined him as a real person before. Someone who watches football or cuts the grass like my dad. I always thought they had to wear their priest outfits and pray all the time.

"Rachel Martin and Carla Varley," Father Kessel says, and I'm thinking I have no idea who Carla Varley is when up walks this girl who I notice is actually wearing make-up on a canoe trip.

"Hi," she says, and I catch the smell of perfume and hairspray riding the hot air.

"Hi," I say, then I recognize her. "Don't we have third hour math together?"

"Yeah, I sit like three seats behind you."

"Sorry. I'm still getting used to all this."

"That's okay. So you didn't go Redemption with any of them either, did you?" she says as she gives the clot of gabbing girls behind her a nod.

I shake my head no. "Parcels Middle School."

"Ligget," she says, "I guess they decided to put the public school kids together."

"Easier to keep an eye on us that way," I say without smiling, but she still laughs.

Father Kessel comes out of the livery fanning himself with his clipboard. He tells us to line up by the door for our paddles and life jackets. "Order girls, be polite, form a line, this way," he says, and they all really do follow him, just like sheep.

"Do you actually know anything about canoeing?" Carla asks as we get in line.

I wave my hand through the little gang of gnats circling my head. "My dad's taken me a bunch of times," I say. "He taught me all the strokes." Then I notice the mosquito bites on the inside of my thigh. Great. I'm sure I'll look awesome covered with a million huge welts when I go swimming over at Ron's after school on Monday—that is if I'm not stuck doing homework.

"You'd better ride in back then," Carla says, "I've only been once, and that was with my boyfriend, so we didn't do much canoeing." She smiles and raises her plucked eyebrows like she's sure I understand.

"Did you bring any bug spray?" I ask her.

"Yeah, my mom gave me some of this aloe lotion repellant stuff that even smells good." She pulls a squeeze bottle out of her back pocket and hands it to me, and I start thinking she might not be half-bad.

After everybody's taken their white floating seat cushions and paddles from the ranger, who I can't help but notice is kind of cute, he makes us go sit in the shade of a wood pavilion near the dock so he can give us what he calls the "rules of the river." But it's way too hot to pay attention. No clouds, giant saw-grass, gnarly mangroves and palms, air that feels like moss when you breathe, a river so shiny with sun I can't even look at it " . . . fatal alligator attack on the Loxahatchee over at Jonathan Dickenson last year. So this river demands our respect and that is why you will stay in your canoes at all times until we have reached the designated disembarking areas . . . " a little green anole sunning itself on one of the pavilion posts. That one I caught when I was little, how he let go of his own tail to escape, left it wiggling in my hand.

When the ranger finishes with the rules, Father Kessel tells us to stand and pray. Like we need to pray so we can go sweat all the way down the river. Everybody signs in. Father turns his palms up, says something about dear Lord Jesus, keep these girls strong in your purpose and help them to see God's wisdom in nature or whatever and on and on he goes until he's just another noise floating off into the background of buzzing bugs and birds singing and the glinting river I glance up at just in time to see a silver fish jump out, spinning and shining wet for a second in the sun before it splashes back down.

For the next few hours I steer us as straight as I can with my J-stroke between swipes at my sweaty, dripping face with the back of my forearm. Less bugs out here on the river, but it's sweat they love, and nice-smelling aloe bug-lotion or not, I've got a little morgue of crushed mosquito bodies, sticky with my stolen blood, lined up on the metal cross-bar where I've smeared them from my palm. So hot. I just want to lean over and fall into the river and float away, all the way back home, right over to Ron's cool pool. At least the heat or maybe the moving around has made my cramps ease up. And then there are the jumping fish and turtles plopping off logs and bright little birds twirling out of the thick, green walls that line the river, and hot as it is, it's really very beautiful.

"How do you like Refuge so far?" Carla asks. "I mean, I'm not sure if I like it or not yet. My mom went there and she said she really loved it and my dad thinks it's a great school where they give you the foundations for success or whatever he calls it and..." My stomach tightens up, sweat drops burn into my eyes, and I smash the mosquito on my knee into a red mess because she's brought me right back to this pack of girls paddling down this stupid, ugly brown river.

"It sucks," I say, "I can't stand it," and then I look over to see the canoe with Father Kessel and the ranger is right along side us.

"Since you two have time for idle talk you've obviously thought out your answers to our lunch-time discussion questions," he says from up in the bow with his paddle across his knees, and I notice he's staring mostly at me.

"Yes, Father," I say as I dig the paddle in and look down at the little trench of muddy water that runs along the canoe's spine.

"Good, Rachel. I look forward to hearing your thoughts."

In the stern, the ranger grins and shakes his head. He seems a lot younger than I thought at first, like twenty-one, and the smirk on his face makes me unsure if he's making fun of me or Father Kessel. Before I have a chance to figure it out, he cuts the water with his paddle and shoots them off toward the head of the pack.

"Did you see the way that cute ranger smiled at us?" Carla says.

Once he's out in front everyone, the ranger turns his canoe upstream in the slow-moving river and points his paddle toward a clearing where there's a long dock running along the shore and another pavilion. "To your right is the Dickenson picnic area," he calls out, "We'll be stopping there for lunch. Pull up to the dock and stay in your canoes until I come by to help you disembark." All at once the other girls start paddling for the dock. I tell Carla to wait, show her how to hold water the same way the ranger was doing. We sit near the center of the river watching the rest of them bumping sterns and bows, scraping the canoes against each other, pinning their own paddles between gunwales as they splash their way toward the dock in a stupid wad.

"Patience, girls," Father Kessel is saying over the noise as he lets the ranger help him climb out of their canoe. "Form a line, form a line," he tells them, walking up and down the dock, wiping his face with a bandanna. One at a time, the ranger helps them out then ties the bowlines of their canoes to the dock posts.

After he's done with the last of them, I sweep my paddle in a big half circle to turn the bow and hope he sees. Carla's right. He is good-looking. Tall like Ron who's already seventeen, but not as skinny. I tell Carla to stop paddling, and I see the ranger is watching me as I angle our nose toward the dock, cut the slow turn to starboard, then ease us in so smooth the port side barely kisses the wet edge of the wood as we stop.

*I look forward to hearing your thoughts.* What a jerk. How stupid can it get, having to stand up in front of everybody and explain why Jesus is important to your life? "Because he loves me if I love him, no matter where I go or what I do. Even when

I'm wrong." That stumped him alright. And then that sandwich. Warm bologna and cheese. Oh my God. No way, I'd barf that up in a second. Raisin cookie wasn't bad, though, and when no one was looking I took a few extra for later. But my stupid watch says it's five o'clock and it's still way too hot and the ranger's already told us we won't be seeing the cabins for another couple of hours. At least Carla's finally caught on. She's taking what my dad would call "good, clean strokes," one hand on the pommel, the other low down on the paddle's shaft. She agrees staying way out in front of the pack is the only way to keep Father Kessel off our asses. She looks over her shoulder for the first of the canoes to come into view around the green bend of the river behind us. Paddling hard has cost her the make-up, which is getting kind of blotchy around her eyes, but I'm not going to say anything about that.

"You got a boyfriend, Rachel?" she asks before she turns back to paddling.

I think about Ron and that time in the basement at the very end of summer. He made no promises. I wonder if I let him touch me as my own promise of something more, a trick to keep his mind on me until I came back for him.

"Yeah," I lie.

"What's he like?"

I don't answer her right away. I put my paddle across my lap and start to think of ways to try and tell her about his tan skin and long black hair and almost spooky blue eyes, and then I realize how everybody's probably still over at his house right now, splashing around and having fun. I know the games they're playing. I can hear their laughter. When I get home tomorrow evening, too late for anything, Laurie will call and say it was no big deal. It was boring. She'll leave out the part about how they stole a couple of Ron's dad's beers or watered down some of his booze, that she cornered Ron in the basement where she touched him after they chugged a Michelob. In the dark on the floor of my room, I'll listen to the truth inside what she doesn't say, and I'll know it should have been me instead.

"Hey, aren't you steering us anymore?" Carla yells and I look up just in time to watch us run aground on a half drowned tree trunk not too far from the mangrove bank. "Shit. We've got to get off this thing before Father Kessel sees us," Carla says, "My dad's gonna kill me if I get another detention."

"C'mon, help me push us off," she says, and before I can tell her to wait she steps from her seat onto the slick log and slips and disappears, comes up a couple seconds later all grimacing like she's in pain, and she's spitting water, thrashing around like crazy, "Oh my God," she screams, "It's got my leg, it's got my leg" and I'm about to start yelling for help when she laughs and stands up in the waist high water instead of going under again.

"Got ya," she says, and I am pissed, but yes she did get me good and this is the first time I've seen anything close to funny out of any of these girls and I start laughing and she starts splashing me and the water is so nice and cool I splash her back until we're both soaked and laughing and barely able to hear Father Kessel who's just made it around the bend in the river screaming, "I said you girls stop that foolishness right now."

The sun is getting low, cutting in glimpses through the trees and glinting off the nearby river as the ranger gets a bonfire going in the pit at the campground. His hair is black like Ron's, but not nearly as long, and I can see a pale scar curling down from behind his ear and along his neck and away under his t-shirt, and he has thick, veiny forearms and hands same as my dad's. He knows what he's doing. He's made a teepee of the twigs packed under with tinder and boxed them in with good kindling. The fire catches quickly, rises up, crackling. Once it's going good he taps a loose log with his boot and bits of red ember rise above his head and drift away. All around I hear whispers and giggles, and I know the others have noticed him, too.

"Time for vesper meditation, girls" Father Kessel says as he steps into the clearing from the trail that leads off to the cabins, "Everyone take a seat around the fire." The twenty or so girls break off from their little groups and find places for themselves on the sandy ground. Carla sits down next to me, looks around to make sure no one's watching, then tilts her head, closes her eyes, and makes a fake snoring sound. I'd like to laugh, only I don't because I'm not sure if we got lucky earlier or not. The ranger pushed us off the log and told Carla not to get out of the canoe again, and Father Kessel looked totally pissed, but I swore it was an accident, which it was, I guess, and he didn't say anything about detention, though that doesn't mean we won't be getting them.

The evening is cooler, and the sand is cool on my legs, and back away from the mangroves, where we are, a wide field of sawgrass gives way to tall cypress and pine as the evening grind of bugs comes on. Father Kessel tells us all to close our eyes and relax, and I try even though I end up squinting through my lashes to watch the ranger play with the fire and the sun sinking red-pink behind mangroves across the river, which is turning blue-black in the dusk.

Father Kessel wants us to "Meditate on the mystery of the Holy Spirit and the power of Jesus' love for our imperfect bodies and souls." I can't see him, but I can hear his voice traveling around the outside of our circle toward me. He's going on about how little Jesus asks in return for the incredible gift of eternal life, how far we've fallen from the perfection God has planned for us, how we are "so susceptible to sins of the flesh."

Then he stops. From behind my back I hear him breathe out a long sigh like he knows there's something he can never beat waiting out there in the night. "You girls are entering a time in your lives where you'll have to make a lot of difficult decisions," he says, "You need to remember to always trust in Jesus who suffered and died so we might live." Then his voice begins to move again as he walks on. "I want you to think about the Lord Jesus right now," he says, "I want you to imagine him like he's someone you know, a friend of yours, sitting there next to you right now talking about the power of God's love."

I try to imagine this, my friend Jesus like a hippie with his long hair and beard and dirty bare feet and worn-out robe. He's got a beautiful smile.

"Tell him how you feel," Father Kessel goes on. "Tell him what you won't tell anyone else. Ask him to help you if you feel confused or lost. He'll always listen."

Jesus takes my hand and my body gets warm. He tucks a strand of his long hair behind his ear and leans over. "I've been watching you," he whispers. He kisses my forehead. Looks into me. He has Ron's startling eyes. "No matter what happens, I'll always love you," he says into mine.

And right then something in my belly peels away, a cramp shoots across my hips, and I open my eyes, pop up to my knees like my spine is on a hinge. The sun is below the trees now, it's darker in the clearing where we are, but the sky is still streaked with red-pink swirls. Father Kessel stares me down from across the fire, his face a scary puzzle of highlights and long shadows, the way a kid's is when he holds a flashlight up under his chin.

"Another problem, Rachel?" he asks, without bothering to try and sound nice about it. Behind him, I can see the ranger sitting with his back up against the trunk of a tree. He's whittling a stick with his knife and he's got that same smirky grin on his face.

"I have to go to the bathroom," I say, "like, right now." Father Kessel lets out a hrummph and looks up at the sky for a second before he turns to the ranger. The ranger stands, walks toward the mouth of the trail that leads away from the clearing. He flicks on his flashlight. "This way," he says, pointing up the trail with the beam. I walk over to him. All the girls watch me as I go past, and I want to look down at myself and check for the blood I'm almost sure is there, but I'm afraid looking will only make it happen. The ranger hands me the flashlight. "Just follow the trail back to the cabins," he says, "You'll see the outhouses about halfway down on your right. You can't miss them."

Once I get out of sight, I'm practically running down the trail toward the outhouses. I rip open an outhouse door, pull down my shorts and shine the beam into my underwear and across my thighs, then I check myself, but there's no blood anywhere. I sit down on the wooden seat. Goddammit, I can't stand any more of this stupid waiting, this stupid trip, all this Jesus talk. How am I supposed to know what Jesus means to me? I'm fourteen, and I can't even have my period like I'm supposed to, like Laurie and all my other girlfriends already do. They're probably all at the roller-blade park or the movies or the mall by now, maybe even still at Ron's house watching something funny on the VCR, maybe under blankets, hands crawling around. Shit. And I'm about to slap the wood wall with my fist when I feel something tickling my shin. I swing the light, catch the tickle in the glare, it's the biggest, ugliest, spider I have ever seen.

"Jesus, Rachel," says Carla, a few hours later, when we're almost alone in our cabin, sitting cross-legged on my bunk playing Gin, "We could hear you screaming like the whole way back to the fire pit." She shakes her head, smiles again, "You may not be big on boobs, but you sure got lungs," and she covers up her mouth with her cards to hide her laughing. "I thought Father Kessel was gonna blow a nut."

"That's not true," one of the sheep says, "He was concerned. He's only trying to do what's best for us. He cares is all."

"Yeah, he cares so much he needs to talk to my dad when we get back tomorrow just to make sure I'm alright," I say. I won't be doing any swimming over at Ron's this week. I wonder if it's okay to hate a priest. Carla snorts and shakes her head. In a way, I can see how the whole thing is funny—my scream ballooning out until I'm there by the edge of the circle of firelight, panting, "Spider. Huge, spider," while I try to catch my breath. Everyone laughing. Father Kessel's angry red face.

"You shouldn't talk about him like that," the sheep, Melissa, I think her name is, says with wide eyes as she zips up her backpack. "It's a sin," and she walks out the door to go find the rest of them, probably all ganged up in the other cabins, talking about us, about me.

"Rummy," Carla says, and she lays all her cards down, "you need to pay attention if you want to win."

"I don't care," I say, and it comes out sounding kind of bitchy even though rummy isn't what I mean.

"That's okay. We don't need to keep score," Carla says as she scoops up the cards and starts to shuffle. Suddenly she stops, gets off the bunk, looks around the cabin and at the tops of the other three bunk beds to make sure we're alone.

"So how far do you let him go?" she asks as she sits back down and starts dealing.

"Who," I say.

"Your boyfriend," she says, "You said before you had a boyfriend. Have you touched him, yet? Is it big? Gary's is big,"

"He's got a huge pool," I say.

"What's his name?"

"Ron."

We pick up our cards.

"Ron. Sounds sexy. I bet he wears one of those little speedo suits, doesn't he?" she says. "You probably go swimming over there all the time."

I nod, look down at the cards in my hand.

"I bet he's really cool, I'd like to meet him," she says and starts to deal. "We should double date or something. My parents go out of town a lot and it's just me and my older brother. He's a Senior at Catholic Central, you'd like him. All my friends from Eisenhower think he's cute. He's even got a fake ID."

I hear what she's saying, but I'm thinking of that last time I was in Ron's pool and what he told me about the boy scout once I explained I wouldn't be over this weekend because I had to go to some lame retreat on the Loxahatchee river. "It was like a year ago," he'd said in the deep end where we floated by ourselves, our legs hanging halfway off a rubber raft we'd turned sideways. "The kid was in my cousin's friend's troupe. Stepped out of the canoe into the shallows to goof around and BOOM the gator took him by the leg and drug him off. Gone. Just like that. BOOM," and he grabbed me and we slipped off the raft and under the water slapping and tickling at each other until we came up to the surface laughing.

"What's the matter, Rachel? Did I say something wrong?"

"You shouldn't have gotten into the river. You heard what the ranger said about the alligators. Something bad could've happened. We still might end up getting detentions."

"Oh, come on," she says and tosses down her cards, "that was the most fun anybody had all afternoon and you know it. Can't you tell how jealous they all are? None of them had the guts to do that. You come to the party my brother and me are planning on throwing once my parents leave for Europe next month. Now that'll be dangerous," she says and picks her cards back up, "We got a pool too, you know."

A few hands later the cramps are back and I start to rock a little and fold my arms across my stomach.

"I don't feel so hot," I say. "I think maybe I should go to bed."

"You got cramps? Getting your visitor, huh," Carla says and she breathes out and shakes her head like she's been through it a million times already. "Sucks, but it's better than having to worry about being late."

"I think I need to lay down."

"Okay, that's cool," she says and gets up off my bunk. "Maybe I'll go see if that ranger's still hanging around the fire pit. He's probably getting pretty lonely by now." She smiles, gives me a goofy wink, "See you later."

"Yeah, see you later," I say as I crawl inside my sleeping bag with my clothes still on. I wonder how far she's really let her boyfriend go. I think about the visitor like it really is some mysterious person. A woman in a red suit who keeps showing up. Sometimes when you want her to, sometimes when you don't. Next to my bed. "Believe it, I'll be back," she says and spreads open the walls of my mouth and climbs down inside me. The visitor. I don't remember my mom ever calling it that. Cramps shoot, burn like stars across my black insides. Too hot in this bag. Too hot. I crawl back out and lie on top. Let the bugs have another chance. Feel one on my shin already, sticking that needle in—too tired and achy to smash him. Mom. How does she put up with this? Now I get why she went on the rampage every month. No wonder her and Dad couldn't get along—but that's not true—they used to. Sunday mornings, squeaky bed, muffled voices coming from their room. She'd pop out into the hallway humming, smile at me. Smell of bacon in the kitchen, Dad flipping pancakes. Church after breakfast and I'm ten right between them kneeling on the dark red kneelers of incense-smoky St. Ambrose, where the priest holds the host up above his head, out to me, away from the giant statue of crucified Jesus pinned to the wall by floodlight nails. Seems like such a long time ago. Haven't thought of Jesus much since. At least not until lately. Jesus. Always looks so tired, head leaning to one side, crown of thorns, made fun of and whipped and stabbed, eyes rolling back, slack mouth right on the verge of shouting, "Enough already!" and his hands rip off the nails to grab the hammer out of that soldier's hands and bash him in the face with it. Tired. Way too tired for that. Splash holy water from the big marble fonts on the painted blood dripping from the wounds, wash yourself, water a little salty like sweat dripping down my forehead after making the sign of the cross on my way out, dripping down, washing off the blood, so hot, even in the dark....

...and the sky barely graying into dawn when my eyes snap open, and above the soft, steady breathing of the other girls my body is telling me what I finally know for sure: the visitor is here.

I grab a fresh Kotex Thin from my backpack and shove it into the back pocket of my cutoffs. When I stand I see Carla is sleeping on the top bunk, her face turned toward the wall. I leave her there, snoring quietly, and go outside.

Across the river the tips of the mangroves glow like matchsticks, but the moon is somehow still out, bluing the darkness, and I head down the trail toward the fire-pit because I will not go into that outhouse again. Up ahead I can see the embers of the fire in the pit in the clearing, then a shadow blocks the mouth of the trail. I think about stepping off into the sawgrass where I won't be seen, but a beam of light pegs me to the spot, and there I am shading my eyes with my hand and blinking.

"Up a little early, aren't you?" the ranger says.

"When you gotta go..." I say.

He snaps off his flashlight. "Don't want to use that outhouse, eh? Can't blame you there," he says, "Never use it myself. Doesn't seem right, somehow. Best to be natural."

Then he just stands there, outlined in the ember light from the fire he's had going all night, smoke rising behind his head. My heart starts beating fast. I don't know if I want to run away or toward him.

"Follow me," he says and waves me along. I follow him across the clearing, where I see his sleeping bag, thrown open and laid out by the fire, then off into the saw-grass. A warm breeze blows across us, and I stay close, inhaling his wood-smoke smell, watching his beam of light swing back and forth as he picks a path through the half-dark. I trip on a rock or a log, start to fall. His strong hand shoots out, grabs my arm, and he pulls me up again.

"Watch yourself," he says, squeezing gently before he lets me go.

We walk on. I can't help wondering what it would feel like for him to touch me again, pull me close with his calloused hands. Was he alone when Carla found him? What did they talk about? Me? Suddenly he stops, turns, and I almost crash right into his chest. We're in another little clearing near the river. The water gurgles as it goes past. I can smell bitter coffee on his breath.

"This okay?" he asks and moves his flashlight in a circle around us. I'm about to tell him it's fine when a strange barking sound comes to us from far away.

"Alligator," he says, "Don't worry, they're more afraid of us than we are of them. Just got to watch for those nesting females."

He points his beam down the shoreline a little ways, catching the edge of the river, black and gliding under the fading moon. "I'll be right over there. Give a holler when you're done."

He turns his back on me, walks off towards the river's edge. I yank my cutoffs and underwear down and squat, surrounded by the tall, silvery grass. In the moonlight I catch a faint whiff of iron and I can see the dark smear on the old pad. I take it out, set it on the ground, open and peel the back off the sticker on the new pad then stick it to the crotch of my underwear. I stand, slide up my underwear and shorts. I don't know what else to do with the old pad but bury it in the sand.

Finally. I feel like someone's let me out of myself. "Don't worry, it will happen," my mom said. Now it has. I see my own body, mine to own, bare feet planted solid on the sandy ground, bony heels strong enough to smash the skull of a snake. I think about Ron who's asleep right now. Later, when the sun is up, I'll find what I need to bring him. Pearly piece of shell. Flamingo bone. Shed of snake skin. Something like I doubt he's ever seen. Ron. I'll make his heart pound with mysteries.

Something small rustles behind me in the grass. Something scared, not scary. I stare at the spot, and it turns still. I look for the ranger. He's standing by the water's edge, searching the river with the beam of his flashlight. I want to go over there and stand next to him and help him spot whatever he's looking for. I want to be the one to point into the dark river, whisper, "Look, an alligator," as his light touches those reptile eyes as bright as God's intentions.

# Rest Stop

Wicklow was trying to take a crap in a filthy Alabama rest stop: knife-scarred graffiti stall, overflowing trash can, floor sticky with who knew what—but he was alone, which was all he ever wanted out of a public restroom. Wicklow's wife, Maura, and Wicklow were on their way back from a cheap beachside Florida motel where they'd made a wreck of the week drinking too much and ignoring their problems, the latest being this throbbing retreat north made in a black Ford Escort with crank windows and a broken air conditioner.

Right before the rest stop they'd been arguing about the wind. Specifically, the windows. "Goddammit, up," or "Fuck that, down." "Goddammit up," because the wind kept whipping her dyed red hair out of its ponytail and into her mouth. "Fuck that, down," because it was pushing ninety degrees outside and Wicklow was still sweating out the bourbon from their last night at the motel—a night where they had both drunk more than enough to repeatedly lose track of what, exactly, they were arguing about before passing out. The hex of that bad vibe had followed them from the beach, down the highway, and into the empty parking lot of this rest stop just south of Montgomery where Wicklow had left her scowling in the car.

Now Wicklow sat in the handicapped stall, pants down and straining, fed up to here with a world in which he couldn't even take a decent crap. He knew this withholding of relief was personal, some kind of payback for everything and then some. He pushed angrily and groaned with red-faced hatred for his own body, finally forcing some pitiful result. Just as the bathroom door slammed open to clench him up again.

Two pairs of motorcycle boots scuffed across the cracked tiles. Leather squeaked. Belts jangled. Piss hit porcelain.

"Hoo wee! What the fuck! Goddamn rat crawled up somebody's ass and fuckin' died, man."

Drawling laughter. "I hear that."

"Shee-it. Some motherfucker got something seriously wrong with his fuckin' ass."

"Fuck off, rednecks."

The words were bunched up inside Wicklow's mouth, cinched behind the ring of his tightened lips and on the verge of piling out, when he imagined the stall door kicked in, his face shoved into the toilet. So he held back, considered the false play at cool. "Been riding hard and put up wet, boys." Then he realized saying something like that would probably get his ass kicked, too. He decided to say nothing at all, acting as if he somehow hadn't heard what all three of them knew he must have heard. He even stilled his breath, waiting in silence as they zipped, mumbled a few things and left, laughing at what Wicklow tried to convince himself was something else.

When Wicklow gave up and came out of the bathroom she was gone. Along with the car. There were only the two beefy bikers leaning against their hogs. Looking at Wicklow looking around in shock at the otherwise empty parking lot. Listening with smirks on their faces as Wicklow explained his sorry self and asked for a ride. Grinning at each other and shaking their heads as the bigger of the two thumbed for Wicklow to get on back, and Wicklow swinging his leg over the bitch seat and putting his arms around the man's thick waist. Wicklow having to lean into that biker's back, smell the rank leather, hold on and hope the wind wouldn't tear him loose as that motorcycle lurched through its gears and after her.

# The Way I See It

No, I can't tell you the date. I get two days off every seven, and the off days change with the post assignments. Between that and working third shift as a vacation relief I'm lucky if I remember what day of the week it is.

I'm thinking it was in July. That's when they had me over at Stamping.

The time? Yeah, I know the time. Everything we do, we gotta do at a specific time. You fuck up the time, you're gone. Had to be right around midnight because I was just starting the midnight fire route when I last saw her.

The fire route? Same as walking the rounds, except you got this big leather clock looks something like a giant hockey puck with a keyhole in it, and there's all these keys hanging off chains around the plant, and you walk the route to a key then pop the key into the hole and give it a crank to mark this spool of paper inside that's getting time stamped as the clock runs.

I'm not sure if they keep the spools. I guess they do in case they want to compare the time stamps with the key marks to see where you were when if there's been a fire or something.

So I was at the first key, which is outside the main door of the plastics warehouse right there on Factory Drive when a car pulled up across the street in front of the Hi-Lo.

The make? I'm not sure. Some kind of sedan. Blue maybe.

The Hi-Lo? It's the bar directly across from the south gatehouse on the corner of Factory and Eight Mile.

Yes, it's popular with the auto plant workers, it's right across the street. Look, are you gonna let me talk or are you gonna keep asking me questions every five seconds?

Okay. I was hitting the first key and I saw this car pull up in front of the Hi-Lo and she gets out and starts yelling at whoever's in the car, telling him to go fuck himself or whatever.

How do I know it was a guy in the car? I don't know, I guess I just assumed. She's a prostitute. It wasn't one of her girlfriends, man.

Fine. I'll stick to what I know for sure.

So she's standing at the curb laying into whoever's inside, and I was about ready to go to the end of the drive and put the Mag-lite on them, just to let them know I was around. Then I decided, whatever, none of my business, and I walk on.

I don't know what happened next. Second key is through the door inside the plastics warehouse, so I didn't see what she did, but that was the last time I saw her. She wasn't there when I got back from the route, but she was usually gone by then anyhow.

I told you I don't know the date. It was the first night of that weird cold snap we had. That was July, right? I remember I didn't have my uniform jacket with me at work. I mean, who needs a jacket in July? But it was cold as hell, man. Before I went on the route I was sitting there in the booth with the space heater on thinking about having to go out there and freeze my ass off while I watched her pace up and down the street hugging herself, and I started thinking, damn, she looks miserable. She wasn't getting much action, probably because of the weather. I thought about giving her the sweatshirt I had in my car, but I knew that was a bad idea. I mean you don't leave your post unless you're going on a route. That's rule number one. And I need this job. I got all kinds of bills.

No I didn't see her again. I was off the next day and then they posted me somewhere else, Mound Road Engine maybe, I'm not sure. You'll have to check that with my supervisor. Like I said I get bounced around a lot because I'm vacation relief and I got no seniority.

How long? She was there the whole two weeks. Usually came out of the Hi-Lo about ten. First time I saw her, I had no idea she was a prostitute. She was wearing regular clothes, you know, a t-shirt, acid washed jeans, Members Only jacket, those wrinkly ankle high boots, not like any sleazy stuff. She was carrying a sparkly little purse. You'd think she was clerking for shipping or receiving to look at her.

Well, it didn't take too long to figure out. She'd cock her hips and wave or turn around and shake her ass every time a car turned the corner. Once they'd pulled over, she'd stand there, playing friendly but really being suspicious on the curb, scoping out the interior, trying to make sure it wasn't one of you guys or whatever before she got in. Acting like that, what else could she be?

Off toward the dark end of Factory Road. She was doing maybe two guys an hour in the time I watched her between ten and twelve. Then I'd go on the midnight route and she'd be gone when I got back, like I said.

No. There was nobody coming in or out of my gate. The whole south end of the factory was down for change-over. They're switching models. Going from economy jobs to some big ass truck van kinda things, SUVs they're calling them. The machinists were using North. No people, no freight. It was zipped.

The responsibilities were like any post at a down gate. You drink coffee, walk the routes, watch the dark. And she was in my dark.

Well, I can't say I enjoyed watching her, no. It was tough to look at, I mean she's selling herself and everything, but what else was there to do? Factory's down, nothing's coming in or out. And that's my job, to keep an eye on things, to watch, right?

I guess I found it interesting in a sad kind of way. I'd never seen an actual prostitute at work before. It just started hitting me in a different place after I sat there for a few nights seeing her rack up the men like that. All those guys picking her up and dropping her off. A different guy in every car. You end up thinking about what they're doing to her. I mean, that's dangerous for all kinds of reasons. Especially these days with the AIDS thing.

Yeah, prostitution is illegal, I should have come to you sooner, said something to my supervisor, right. I know. But I didn't see anybody pimping her or beating on her. Far as I could tell she was just selling what she had and doing what she could to get by. It's none of my business what's going on in her life. For all I know she had some kid who depended on her. And there she was selling her ass to survive. That's gotta make you feel pretty low. Like she needed to be arrested on top of all that.

Look, and I want to be perfectly clear on this—I never actually saw her doing anything illegal. All I ever saw was her getting into and out of people's cars.

Whatever. I just noticed the article in the paper and thought she looked something like the girl in the picture and decided to come in and tell you what I know. I mean, it's probably not even her. I'm just saying.

No. I haven't been posted to Stamping since.

Go there when I'm off? Why? What, you think I'm some John? Fuck that. I don't pay for it.

3<sup>rd</sup> Precinct: 9/23/87

I come in trying to help you guys find a missing person and you call my supervisor and tell him some bullshit so I get a random sprung on me where I piss dirty and catch an indefinite suspension without pay. Then you show up at my apartment and drag me down here for questioning. And you wonder why nobody ever wants to talk to the cops.

My brother? Yeah, he's the one who got his arm mangled in a press over at the News a few months back. So what? Why you gotta bring my little brother into this?

Had he been acting suspicious? Well, he wasn't acting normal. He'd just had his arm cut off. How would you be acting?

Was he on my mind while I was at work? Let's see. Best bass player in the city gets his arm gets sucked into a press and smashed to mush. Some guy from RCA at his last gig before the accident talking about a recording contract. Out of the hospital two weeks and his band tells him sorry but they have to get a new bass player, they hope he understands. I was supposed to be road manager. It was going to be goodbye gate houses. Now he won't hardly talk to me. I have to drag him to the hospital so they can teach him how to use his prosthetic arm. And I got no help. Dead parents. An ex and a kid and out West. Yeah. He was on my mind.

Well you already know I smoke weed now, don't you? My super does, too, thanks to you.

Did I ever smoke on shift. No. Only when I'm off.

You don't have to believe me. It doesn't change what I told you.

NO. I'm telling you I have no idea what happened to her. Last time I saw her, she was standing outside the Hi-Lo talking to some guy in a car and then I went on to the next key. She was gone when I got back, like I said.

Yeah. I guess it is kind of weird that there are missing key prints on the spool from the midnight fire route on the night I'm talking about. I don't know why. The clocks malfunction sometimes.

Alright. Okay, fine. I didn't walk the twelve o'clock that night.

I just needed to relax, man. It was my last night at that post so I smoked a bowl in the plastics warehouse right after I hit the first key. I mean, my brother's all fucked up, my wife's taken my boy away, the woman across the street has to sell her ass to live, and I'm guarding a down factory in a dying town. It was too much.

I don't know. For some reason she was the one thing I couldn't stop thinking about. I started wondering where she lived or if she had a pimp or a boyfriend or whatever. If she ever got slapped around. I started thinking about her life beyond the street. Like what about her family? Did she maybe have kids she was trying to take care of? A habit she wanted to kick? I mean, obviously her life was all screwed up, but maybe all she needed was somebody to help pull her out of the shit. Somebody who cared a little.

No. That's not what I'm saying. What I'm saying is by the time I got back to the booth I'd worked myself into this weird kind of worry over this woman I didn't even know. Which is why I couldn't tell you the rest before, because why would you believe that I cared about her at all? You'd think I just wanted to fuck her, or worse, considering what's happened, and if I admitted I was high and all the rest, well, look what you already did to me.

No. I did not pick her up.

I'm telling you what actually happened. I was coming out of the plastics warehouse at about quarter to one, walking to the booth after blowing off the route, thinking this stoned jumble of shit about everything going wrong when this car pulls up and she gets out and says whatever to who's inside like I told you. That's the same. What's different is it's not midnight, it's twelve forty-five, and I'm not starting the route, I'm coming back from it, but I hadn't really walked it anyhow, I'd just been sitting in the plastics warehouse, getting stoned and thinking.

Well then the car drove off toward the dark end of Factory, and there she was standing alone across the street, which surprised me because she'd always been gone when I got back before. Then I noticed she was staring at me. And that really freaked me out because she hadn't looked my way once the whole two weeks, even though I'd been watching her, and now she finally does it when I'm totally stoned so I'm not even sure if she's actually looking at me or not. Once she sees I'm looking back at her she starts waving, like waving me over, so I walked down to the edge of the drive to ask her is everything okay.

And she said, sure, unless you rentals got issues with working girls.

I told her I didn't have issues with working girls.

And she said, well, why don't you come on over and take me for a ride then.

I could see she was amped up on something, tweaking, touching her face a lot and scratching her arms. I told her I had some clothes she could wear if she was cold.

She said no, she wasn't cold, she was fine.

I wasn't having it. She was not fine. I told her to hold on a minute. I figured they want to fire me for having a conscience, whatever. I went to my car parked behind the booth, got out the sweatshirt then left my post and walked across the street and handed it to her, and I said, really, put it on, and she said thanks, maybe later and tied it around her waist.

I said she could come into the booth to warm up if she wanted. I had the space heater. I didn't care if I lost my job. I was sick of people turning their backs on each other.

She laughed and said no way was she getting into some guard booth with me, but I should come by off duty some time, she'd give me an employee discount. Then she told me she needed a drink before last call, and she went into the Hi-Lo.

I have no idea what happened to her after that. Next day I had off, then I got sent to Mound Road or wherever.

What do you mean it doesn't add up? Believe what you want, I don't care.

A suspect. Is that so? Then I'm done talking until I get my phone call.

I set my empty beer glass down on the countertop scarred with little brown-black burn craters from the factory rats who've decided not to bother with the flimsy tin ashtrays. There's a TV hanging in the corner above the electric dart machines: a commercial for some cable channel with clocks and letters of the alphabet zipping through outer-space, weaving their way through fields of asteroids and around planets with rings. At the end of it all comes a close-up of a woman's terrified face, her painted lips, the O of her mouth freezing into a silent scream. She seems familiar somehow, maybe from an old movie Zane and me caught some late night on Count Ghoulio when we were kids.

I glance down to the far end of the counter, across the faces. She's watching the TV, too, and I look away before she notices my stare. I don't see my sweatshirt. I can't help wondering what she might have traded it for.

"You're on," somebody says, then comes the sharp snap of the cue ball exploding the rack. A bearded, beer-gutted guy rubbing chalk on the end of his stick circles the rails, his beer gut hanging down below his dirty t-shirt. "You are so fucked," he says to someone, and before I turn away he bends over to shoot I get flashed by his hairy back and the hairy crack of his hairy ass. Beer commercial comes on: platinum blondes in white bikinis ready to do anything at the twist of a bottle cap; it's a re-run, some fantasy about getting your wish and hanging around with the Scandinavian Swimsuit team. I give a short wave to catch the bartender's eye, tap my wedding ring against my empty beer bottle as I slide it across the counter. Think about a whole world hooked on need.

The beers go down as I go over the fight with Zane. I tongue the cut on the inside of my lip from where a tooth sliced when he used his good arm to club me with his fake one. Gonna have a nice bruise on my face tomorrow. The whole idea of it pulls a bitter chuckle out of me—getting slapped down with a fake arm. But I didn't have the money for one of those new, realistic looking things. So I got Zane the old kind, a piece of hard, flesh-colored plastic with metal pincers where the hand and fingers should be. Glad he didn't club me with that end.

The laugh turns sick in my stomach. I consider another shot. I can't imagine what it must feel like to have part of you suddenly caught like that, trapped outside of your control and squeezed into mush inside a machine while you can still feel. I imagine him standing there, screaming, flailing around for the kill switch, a thing I'm thankful I did not have to see.

The door was unlocked at his apartment when I showed up earlier tonight; I came in on him fresh out of the shower and offered him a beer. When he grabbed for the can, his towel came loose, and the stubbed right arm started moving to gather it up like there was still an elbow, a forearm, a hand attached. "Goddammit, you could've at least opened it," he yelled, and he threw the beer to the floor and bent to snatch the towel up over his crotch again.

"It's not like I never seen you naked before," I said, and I set another unopened can down on the sink as I walked out and went to the kitchen to fridge the rest of the twelve pack. That hospital psychologist told me he had to learn to cope.

Zane was on morphine pills for what they call residual limb pain, and after a few beers and some weed he was higher than I'd seen him in a while—my little bro who used to go shot for shot with the hard-core crowd at Jumbo's back when he was still in high school. Now he was teenage blasted again from the mix of beer and pills and weed, sloppy drunk out of control like he'd get at fourteen when I started letting him tag along for keg parties and cruising Gratiot in the Camaro.

"I know what this is, Les," he said. "Feel-good mission. Make the gimp forget his bummer. Well, fuck you. I don't want it." He pushed his way up from the couch and stood, unsteady, staggering a little as he tore loose the straps that held on the arm, which he then grabbed by the wrist and yanked off. I was still waiting on the one-liner, the funny face, any of the things he used to do to cut up a bad vibe—something to show me he was still my prankster little brother Zane. But he just stared at me, looking ready to pitch over like that press had taken his balance along with his arm. "This is me now," he finally said.

"Bullshit," I said. I got out of my chair, put on some Zeppelin, and that flicked his switch.

"Did I say I wanted to hear any music?" he screamed, "NO FUCKING MUSIC," and by the time I turned away from the stereo to tell him to lighten up, he was already on me, prosthetic arm coming down hard. I fell back against the stereo, knocked over his milk crate full of records.

Standing over me, he pulled off his shirt. "See it," he shouted, waving the red, scarred nub of his arm in my face, "Look at it! This is who I am now. Look, fucker!"

I shoved him away hard, too hard, and the coffee table took his legs out from under him, sending him flopping onto the couch.

"You're still my brother," I said as I stood up, "Nothing's changed."

"Don't you get it? There's no more music. NO. MORE. MUSIC." And behind me I could hear Zeppelin skipping, stuck on one note like the band was going to vamp it forever. I slapped the needle off the record and skidded the room into silence.

"That's up to you," I said.

He pushed himself upright. "You think you know what it means to lose something," he mumbled, his anger fading as he searched the floor with his eyes, looking among the fast food wrappers and newspapers and empties for the reason why this had happened to him. "But you don't. You don't know shit."

Only I did know, I knew too well, and what I should've done was grab him by the hair and shove a picture of his nephew into his face, but I didn't.

"I know this girl," I said. "She digs the band. I can bring her by."

"You bring some fucking girl over here and I'll kill her," he said, and he pushed himself up from the couch with his one arm, wobbled down the hall and slammed the door to his room.

She shoots the rest of her drink and stands up from her stool, makes some wise crack to the bartender about squeeze you later, and I feel her pass behind me then on out through the door, trailing a stink of cheap perfume. I drop money on the counter and get up. The pay phones are right there by the jukebox next to the door, and for a second I consider calling Zane, but he doesn't answer his phone these days, and he's probably dead out on the morphine anyway.

The fat guy at the pool table starts talking again. "Take you this game, buddy, I got enough for my girlfriend outside." He reaches a hairy paw over his belly to cup his crotch. Need. I push through the door and out into the night, hear the door slap shut behind me, cutting off the tinny jukebox music.

She turns toward the sound. I walk the other way, off into the parking lot. I want to pretend I don't know why I came here, but I do. I key open the Camaro, get in, turn on the radio, crank up the heat. It's crazy cold for July.

Eighty dollars left in my wallet, money I was ready to blow on my little bro once we hit downtown Detroit. Instead I'm sitting alone in the parking lot of a dive bar warming up the car with a fat cut inside my mouth. I slip the eighty dollars into my left front pocket for easy access. Open the glove box to toss in my wallet. The wallet flips open and shows its insides as it lands. Picture of my little boy Seth right there in the plastic photo insert, watching me. I slap the wallet closed on his face, snap the glove box door shut. He has a birthday coming soon, four on August 3rd, just a few weeks away. His mother is re-married and living in California now, working some cushy marketing job—just one more invisible, missing thing I can still feel. Won't let me see him unsupervised, and I can't afford the time off work or the lawyer to change her mind. I should just drive out there some day and take my boy right out of her yard, just lift him over the chain link fence as he says daddy and raises his arms to me. Bring him back home, take him to Chuck E. Cheese and a Lions game like we used to do. Only I'm not even sure if he'd recognize my face.

The wipers sweep a thin layer of frost off the windshield. I check the clock. 11:50. Guard across the street should be getting ready to go on the route. I adjust the rearview, take one more look to make sure she's still on the corner. Then I pull out and swing the car down the dark alley behind the bar and around the block to Eight Mile.

I take the corner off Eight Mile onto Factory. She's smiling as the car rolls slowly up to the curb, a sexy smile, but fake. Gives me a little wave. I roll the window down and she leans over and looks in, checks out the back seat to make sure I'm alone. From this close she looks younger than I thought. And skinnier. Sick skinny. And no make up, which surprises me, because I figured she'd be wearing too much, but I can still tell she was once pretty in hard way.

"Nice car, " she says. "Blue makes me horny. Can I get a ride?"

I look across the street. The booth is empty. I lean across the seat and pop open the door for her, "Get in. It's cold."

She flops onto the seat, closes the door, starts rubbing her hands in front of the vents while I put in Sprocket's demo tape. My bro's band. Fucking rocks, but I keep it low. She sniffles, wipes the back of her hand across her nose like a little kid then goes into her routine.

"So. You want to party?"

I tell her yeah, definitely and she says, "It's twenty-five for a blow job, forty for straight up, fifty for half and half. Nothing kinky and you wear a rubber no matter what."

I nod along to the jams. I really think these guys will make it. My brother will be left behind. He wrote some of the songs on this tape, songs that are getting them signed, but he won't see a dime.

"You mind turning that down?"

"Sure," I say, and I turn it down a little, but not much.

"Okay, I gotta ask, you a cop?"

"Nope." I say. Then I can't help myself, "Just a rental looking for the employee discount."

"What?" She leans forward, tries to get a better look at me in the green dash light of the dark car. I'm out of uniform, Tigers hat pulled low over my eyes.

"Where's your sweatshirt?" I ask.

"Sweatshirt? What the fuck are you talking about sweatshirt?"

Her pupils, blown wide, reflect the neon of the Hi-Lo's sign. She can't even remember last night. Of course not. I should've known better.

"Do I know you or something? You look kind of familiar." I can smell the liquor on her sour breath. She scratches at her arms, nervous. "You're not a cop, right? I need you to say it."

I look her square in the face. "I am definitely not a cop," I say, and for a second I think she almost recognizes me, then inside the black holes of her eyes I see the thread of whatever memory she's grasping for snap, and the idea of anyone I could be beyond the next forty bucks sinks back into the fucked up mess inside her head.

"Okay. Drive," she says.

"So how've you been?" I ask. "Everything good?"

"Fine. Whatever. Working. Why do you care? You want some ass, you better start driving."

I drop the car into gear, pull away from the curb and drive us slow toward the dark end of Factory.

"Hurry it up, would you? I ain't got all night."

I give it a little gas. "No problem," I say, "Just thought you'd want to sit in the warm for a while."

She's not used to nice and thinks it must mean something else. She goes quiet and keeps her eyes on my hands, which I've hung high on the steering wheel on purpose as I steer toward the dark half of the dead end street.

"Stop here," she says.

I pull beneath a big maple that overhangs the street. With the glow of the one street lamp up the block, we're in the shadow of the night. Now it's just us and the barbed wire fencing surrounding the silent south side of the factory, the dim glow from the Hi-Lo behind. She's nervous-breathing, tapping her fingers on the armrest. I fast-forward the tape to the next song. On comes the slap-bass intro—my bro grabbing it, and the drum roll surging up like boiling water, and the crying sound of feedback as the lead guitar dives in. Sprocket, rocking ass, Detroit style. I crank it, fix the EQ, nod my head along.

"So, what the fuck is it gonna be, man?" She's starting to get pissed off, yelling over the volume. I don't say anything, just keep nodding my head to the groove, and I know it's bothering her that she can't read me. That she can't tell if my not answering means business or danger or something she'll never understand. And it bothers her more that she even needs to hang around long enough to try and figure me out. Need. But I don't mean anything bad. All I want is for her to sit there and pay attention to the song, which is really a fucking kick ass song I know she'd dig if she'd just listen.

I turn the music down. "You like that? Awesome, right? That's my brother's band."

"Man, I don't give a fuck about your brother's band," she says. "I don't have all night to sit around listening to your bullshit." She reaches for her door.

"Wait." I clamp my hand down on her skinny thigh. Just as fast, I realize my mistake and let her loose before she has to tear her leg away. For a few seconds she freezes, hangs there with her fingers curled around the door handle, the other hand ready to go for the blade or whatever she has tucked into those low, wrinkly boots that go over the cuffs of her pants. I look through the windshield at the maple above us, its leaves stirring in the dark breeze, flashing silver as they turn against the streetlight. I can feel her fear, her mind weighing how badly she needs my money against the idea that trying to get out again might only make things worse. I want to say something kind. But I doubt kindness is something she still believes in. Or is it that I don't have anything kind to say?

"I'll take head," I tell her, because I have to tell her something to keep her around, and asking her to just sit with me for a while so we can listen to some music will not make her stay.

"Fine," she says without relaxing at all. "But grab me again and I'll fucking bite it off."

She looks me up and down, making the final decision. "Okay. That's twenty-five up front."

I give her twenty-five. She sticks it in her boot, tells me to unzip and sit on my hands, which I do.

She leans across the seat, pulls me out of my underwear, rolls on a rubber, and goes to work. No warming up, no pretend affection or porn star acrobatics. Just fast and mechanical like I imagine a vacuum cleaner tube full of Vaseline would feel. I have the urge to caress her hair, but I don't dare, and I'm there before the song is even over.

"Take me back now," she says, turning the mirror to check her face as I get myself together.

I swing the car around, drive her back to her corner. She already has the door open and one leg out on the pavement by the time I decide to tell her.

"I know someone else," I say, "My brother over in Harper Woods. He's got an apartment, I think he'd be interested. It'd be an all night gig. There's a couple hundred in it for you." Of course, I don't have a couple hundred, but I'll worry about that if she says yes.

"What do you mean, you think he's interested? He is or he isn't."

"It doesn't matter what he says when we get there, I'll pay you either way. Two hundred bucks. Fifty up front. Right now." I pull out the cash. Show it to her. "We can get a bottle and party. I got some grass. You can even crash there if you feel like it. You don't want to be out here in this cold, do you? C'mon. He'll be into it. We can talk him into it."

The money and the party and a warm place for the night sound good to her, and I know getting laid is exactly what Zane needs. Give him some confidence. Show him his stump doesn't turn the girls off. Once they're done we can talk. Drink. Smoke down. Listen to music. Maybe I can find a way to help her out somehow. When was the last time anybody took her out for breakfast?

"It'll be worth it," I say. "He's a cool guy. This band right here, they just got a record deal. He's gonna be a big star, man. It's just that things have been rough for him lately. I think he needs some . . . you know . . . someone he can get close to who doesn't have to try and understand."

I figure I'll deal with the missing arm like I will the money I don't have—when we get there.

But something's wrong. She's looking past me, through the driver's side window toward the post across the street. There's a flashlight coming out of the booth. 12:02. He's right on schedule.

"I don't think so," she says as she gets out. "Tell your brother to go fuck himself." She says it loud, angry. She's got my twenty-five bucks and she's had enough of me.

Across the street, the guard's beam swings toward mouth of the gate and stops for what seems like too long. Then it cuts off and the guard walks on into the plastics warehouse.

"What're you waiting on? Get the fuck out of here," she says.

Something ugly flares up in me, and I feel like reaching out and dragging her into the car, grabbing her by the scruff of her neck and telling her through my clenched teeth it's time for things to change. But I don't. What I really want is for her to believe me and get back in on her own, then I'll fix everything for all three of us. Call a lawyer and figure out my visitation rights so I can see my son. Find a way to get her clean and help her turn her situation around. Show Zane that article in *Bass Player* about the one-armed guy who's got his bass set up so he can play it by just tapping the fingers of his one hand on the fret board. Get him playing again. Get him back in the band.

I'm straightening all of us out in my head when she notices the little sparkly purse she left on the seat and reaches for it. I understand now that what I say or do later can't matter. I bow my head to the truth, look over at her raw, scratched up stick of a wrist as she leans in, and I begin to mourn all our lives so weak and easily taken.

# Three Ways of the Saw

*for Jon*

I'm at the kitchen sink washing down pills when they bump up my driveway in a blue Chevy pick-up, its bed eaten through with rust so bad I can see past the holes in the body to the frame. The driver, a big, middle-aged man with stubbly cheeks and a ball cap on, throws it into Park. He takes a drag on his cigarette then pulls it from between his lips. My stomach turns over with envy and regret. I think of how long it's been, and part of me rasps with the urge. Four years, eight months, and eleven days I've kept that unopened pack of Lucky Strikes hidden in my freezer. What difference would it make smoking one now?

The driver gets out and clangs the rusty door shut. He jets two gray streams through his nose, drops his cigarette onto my drive and grinds it out beneath his work boot. Then he does something I don't expect: he bends over and picks the butt up, tearing away the nub of burnt tobacco before shoving the filter into the back pocket of his dirty jeans. He starts up my walk, disappearing from the window frame. I hear the doorbell but don't move. Instead I watch the kid he's got with him rummage through the bed of the truck, lifting out gas cans and ropes and chainsaws.

Last week's storm brought the wet-heavy snow too early, weighing down the half-turned leaves, snapping limbs across the state. Now, after yesterday's rain, there's not even enough snow left on the ground to make a goddamn snowball. What's left are the ruined trees. My honey locust among them.

I want it all to just go away, but when the doorbell rings again I know there's no stopping this.

As soon as I open the door, I smell the cigarettes all over him. "Mr. Ashland," he says more than asks.

"You the service," I say.

"That's right, sir. J. W.'s Tree Service. I'm J. W. Good to meet you."

"Here for my honey locust," I say.

"Yes sir. If you'll just sign there, please." He hands me the bid sheet on a clipboard, pointing to the blank line that needs my name. I don't even bother to check the price to make sure it's what he and Beverly agreed to when he came by a few days after the storm.

"We'll have that mess out of here in no time, sir."

"I planted that mess over thirty years ago," I say, forcing myself to look away from my mangled tree. Right down at the pack of Camels in the breast pocket of his work shirt. I was sixty-one last time I smoked. Almost five years since they told me they were taking a lung. All these years short of breath, and there still isn't a day I don't think about having one.

"It's a shame, sir. Beautiful tree."

I stand in the open doorway and watch him head off down the walk to where the kid is crouched pouring gasoline into one of the chainsaws. The kid looks to be at the far end of high school, maybe eighteen, and he's concentrating hard on what he's doing, like there's more than a mess riding on his not spilling the gas onto my driveway. He screws the gas cap down, slides the plastic sheath off the bar and hands the saw to J. W.

who eyes along the chain. Satisfied, J. W. pumps the fuel bulb, pops the choke then sets the saw down, putting his foot through the trigger guard as he pulls at the starter cord. The saw sputters until the motor kicks in and blue smoke rises all around him. He stands and revs it, the pitch winding higher and higher into a jagged whine before he finally eases off the trigger and lets the thing fall into an idle.

For days I've been trying not to look at my ruined honey locust a few yards away in the center of the front lawn, but I have to look now. The trunk is shattered at the main crotch about twenty feet up, so most of the crown with its barely turned leaves is hanging down like a woman bending forward to comb out her long hair. From what Beverly says, it's the same all over town.

But today we're near sixty degrees. The sun's shining. I got squirrels and birds hopping across my lawn. More like late April than late October. Staring up into the empty, blue sky it's hard to believe that the sick snap and groan of that honey locust pulled Beverly and me out of bed and onto the living room couch where we looked through the picture window at the broken branches piling up with falling snow.

J. W. shuts off the saw, sets it on the driveway and unzips the army duffel. He hands hard hats, a climbing harness, leg spikes, and coils of rope to the kid who arranges them side-by-side on the lawn. My chest begins to feel tight, tighter than usual, and I decide I better go back inside.

By the time I reach the bathroom cabinet, I'm wheezing hard. I see my boney face in the cabinet mirror, hairless and grey, and I think about the way all things eventually come apart. Behind that face are my pills—Elavil, M.S. Contin. Pills with names like the ships I sailed on in the Navy. Pills I sometimes take and sometimes kiss and wash down the kitchen sink one at a time, depending on the fuel level in my hope tank.

There's a little container of dental floss next to the sink. I pick it up, snap off a length and start in. *Dying with Dignity*, a book I charged out from the library is on top of the toilet tank. I don't recall ever reading it while sitting there, but I must have brought it in at some point. I don't get through more than a handful of teeth when the ridiculousness of the situation—a dying man flossing while staring at the cover of a death-book he's left on top of the crapper—gives me one of those sad-funny well ain't life a bitch moments I'm long since sick of.

I grab the bottle of oxycontin and go to the picture window where I can look out across the front porch at what's left of my honey locust. Used to be that almost every day when I came home from the paper mill I'd sit on the porch swing for a while and watch its thorny, green branches sway in the wind or its snow-covered skeleton hunkering down beneath the flat winter sky. Trimming the thorns off the trunk and otherwise keeping an eye on it had been my habit ever since I planted it thirty-three years ago to grow into blocking out the transformer and telephone pole behind. But there was more to it than fixing a bad view. There is what we decide to take and what we can give back. There is the grind of the mill and the sulfur stink of stripped logs being processed down to slurry, and there are the trees I've planted on this deep lot, one for each year here, the first of them all now halved and dying in the middle of my front lawn.

I hear a chainsaw's angry buzzing, but smaller this time, higher pitched. J.W. comes into view with the sixteen-incher to take the tops off the hanging half of the crown so the tree will drop right after they face and back cut the trunk. I know my way around a chainsaw, around trees. I should be doing this myself, even though I'm dying. Beverly understands how I feel, which is why she put the call in to the tree service before I was even out of bed the morning after the snowstorm. Part of me wants to go out there and tell them to just cut it along the split and tar the half that's left. It could live. Stranger things have happened. And if it did? Like Beverly would want to stare out at the tar-blacked half of my honey locust for the rest of her days.

J. W. starts going at those torn limbs, the pitch of the saw changing when it bites wood. I'm forgetting to watch my breathing now, and suddenly it feels like someone's shoved their hands up inside my chest, wrapped them around my one lung and begun wringing. It's time to drop the shade on all this, which I do before going to sit on the couch with my pills. There's so much we'd like to avoid. It reminds me of my last visit to the oncologist's office. "I'm sorry," Dr. Greenspan had said, "We've done everything possible." He looked truly torn up, like he'd betrayed me, and I think I felt worse for him than for myself. *I'm sorry.* Imagine having to begin telling someone they're dying with the same two words you'd use to apologize to a stranger you bumped into on the street.

The saw cuts off, the silence after filling a space of its own, and I remember something I read in a *Discover* magazine a few months ago about how matter can never be destroyed, only changed. If this is true it means the whole universe already contains everything that ever was or will be. Which, I suppose, makes us all part of one big thing, or at least all related, all individual yet connected, me and Beverly and Catherine the Great and Nixon and Gandhi and Hitler and Jesus and every frog and tree and pile of dog shit and rubber band and piece of paper ever made. Beverly says this is an ugly and Godless way of thinking, she sure as hell isn't related to any Hitler or dog doo or rubber band. "Honey," I told her, "Don't you see that means I always was and always will be part of you?"

To which she said, "You're a jackass to think you could be anything but always a part of me."

"This shit's thorny as hell." The kid's voice drifts in through the open window. "What's he want done with it?"

Once I work up the energy I suppose I'll have to go out there and tell them.

The night of the storm when Beverly and I sat in the dark on the couch looking out at the locust, we weren't talking about it, but we were both thinking the same thing: that tree is done. Like me. All through my illness, she's always tried to put the brave face on things. A transplant. The latest clinical trials. Ever hopeful. But her hope became resignation in time.

"I liked to imagine you sitting out there in the shade reading your paperbacks after I'm gone," I said.

Her eyes glistened in the blue-white darkness, but she didn't cry. Her voice held, clear and soft as she told me, "So did I."

J. W. cranks up the little Husky and waves me over to the mess of branches hanging down off the totally fucked-up tree. "Let's do 'er," he shouts over the idling motor.

"Right on," I say, springing up with the ropes over my shoulder and his harness and leg-spikes in my hands. We've already cut and humped probably two cords of oak this morning, but the last thing I want is him thinking I'm tired or lazy, because I need this job—the best one I've ever had, way better than driving pizzas or working a gas station register or greasing through shifts in a fast food uniform like most of my friends do. We've been busting ass with all this shit the storm left behind, and I want him seeing how I hold up my end. Not too many guys my age luck onto a crew like this one. And today, with G. L. and Rusty split off on their own to handle the extra work, J.W.'s eye is on me, and that means the better I do, the sooner I get to climb and use the saws.

I set the gear down on the far side of the tree and walk over to watch J. W. top the smaller branches. He works the saw up from the bottom if a branch is touching the ground, and down from the top if it hangs without pressure.

"So you don't pinch the chain," he shouts over the whine.

"I know," I shout back, "You've showed me."

After he's sawed all the tops from the hanging limbs, it's my turn to pull brush mule.

"This shit's thorny as hell. What's he want done with it?" I ask, thinking he probably wants it at the curb for city pick-up, an easy haul twenty feet away.

"Drag the branches up there, back into the scrub," J. W. points at the wooded hill next to the house where I can see a dirt trail leading to a tangled thicket of long-dead cuttings. "Better put on your gloves."

"Will do," I say, turning my back to him and keeping my "buncha goddamn fucking bullshit" under the idle of his saw as I pull on my gloves, grab up the thickest of the thorny limbs by their cut ends and start to drag them away.

By the last load I'm stripped to my dirt-smeared T-shirt, sweat rolling down my scratched and bloody arms as I slip my way up the slick mud-path. I do feel like a goddamn mule, grunting, ripping these long branches through the tight spaces between trees, stepping over and through what I've already dragged to set what I'm dragging now on top of the pile I've made. I stop to catch my breath after. Down the hill, I can see J. W. standing on the porch drinking a cup of coffee, it looks like, and talking to the homeowner, some old guy, who's like eight-hundred and coughing into his fist now and again. I take my work gloves off, tuck them into the back pocket of my jeans and head down there.

"First one I ever planted," the old man says, and J.W. nods in sympathy like we're at somebody's funeral.

Then it's an uncomfortable silence and they're looking at me standing there sweating underneath my grimy baseball hat. I feel drops tickling my nose and wipe my forearm across my face. My muscles got the serious burn going, but I can tell I've still got power to give; it's no worse than two-a-days in pads, and I feel like telling J.W. let's hit it and bang this job out so we can get on to the next client. Because that's what getting paid by the job means—harder you work, more you make an hour. Except this is J. W.'s Tree Service, not Donny's Tree Service, so we do it his way. For now.

"Can I get you something to drink, son," the old man says, "Coffee? Water?" and I think, damn, if I really was his son I wouldn't be worried about a drink, I'd be worried about having to bury his ass. His pupils are blasted like he's on some serious shit. He's got a thin, white, stubbly head of cut cornfield hair, grey, liver-spotted skin, and he's breathing in these short little pants as if he'd been going up and down that hill with me. For a second I think maybe it's my own quick breathing that's got him going, so I make an effort to slow mine down. I suck in a nose-full of the crisp fall air and the whole world smells turned over, new and wet, full of those smells I love, the gas and oil and sharp tang of fresh sawdust that follows us everywhere.

"I'm fine, sir," I say, "Thank you."

"Donny, this is Mr. Ashland," J. W. says, "I just found out he used to work with my dad over at the mill."

"We're all connected," the old man says, looking at me in this spacey way like there's some kind of cosmic magic shit in the idea that he happened to work with Grandpa Joe back when the mill employed half the goddamn town.

"Yes, sir," I say.

"Donny's my half-sister's kid," J. W. says, "Guess you could say he's my apprentice. Just graduated high school last June."

"Got your whole life ahead of you, son," the old man says.

"Yes, sir," I say thinking I'd sure as hell like to get on with it instead of standing here fucking around.

"I'm teaching him the way of the saw," J. W. says, "Trying to give him a real education before he decides to go off to college and learn to be a smartass."

"Measure twice. Cut once," the old man tells me, "That's the way of the saw. You can apply that to anything from choosing your girl to your job."

It's the same old shit. Everybody thinking I need their advice on how to live just because they were once eighteen.

The old man glances over at the totally fucked-up tree we've half cut down and hesitates, "Do you have any tree tar?" he asks.

J. W. starts to get a little nervous. "Well sir, realistically, I don't think there's any way we can...I mean, your wife said she wanted us to..."

"I know. I know. Forget it." The old man starts to turn away. "I guess I better get out of your hair."

"I'm sorry sir," J. W. says, "It was a beautiful tree. Had a lot of years left on it."

"Nice to meet you, sir," I say, and the old man nods and cuts us off with a wave as he turns to go inside.

J. W. drains his coffee cup and sets it down. "Let's get this over with," he says, almost like he's mad about it, and I wonder if I did something to piss him off.

We go over to the tree where I've left the spurs and climbing harness. J. W. steps through the leg holes of the harness before buckling it on around his waist and between his legs. Then he steps into one of the spurs and cinches up the leather straps, winding the leather around the metal spike running along the inside of his shin before buckling it tight. He does the same with the other. I hand him one end of the coil of rope which he loops through the 'beaner hanging off the harness belt. He looks the tree up and down, steps to it and hugs the trunk. He raises one leg and chucks the spur in, then straightens himself up on that leg and digs in with the other. Holding on by one arm and the spurs, he works the flip-line open with his free hand and slips it around the trunk to snap it into the clip on the other side of his belt. "Watch for tangles," he says to me, meaning the rope hanging down from his waist to the ground coil. Then he's climbing, working the spurs and flip-line together until he's way up at the tree's broken crotch.

"Send the little Husky," he says. I grab his rope just above the ground-coil and put the two owl eyes in it then fold them inward, toward each other, to make the butterfly hitch in a single line just like he showed me. I wrap the loop around the body of the smaller Husquevarna chainsaw and make it tight. "All you," I call up to him.

He reels the saw in, frees it from the rope, starts it in one pull then begins cutting down on the shattered base of the hanging fork we've already topped. Sawdust floats toward me like golden snow, and I step back. We keep this pace we'll knock out one, maybe even two more jobs today. That's a hundred and fifty bucks at least I'll be taking home for eight hours work, almost six hundred for the week. More than enough to start saving for my own chainsaw and climbing gear; more than enough to buy beer and gas the old 'Stang so Carol Anne and I can go to the bonfire at the lake tonight and work toward that promise she's been giving me in installments, as the two of us like to say.

J. W. finally cuts most the way through the limb, and it creaks like an old door as it slowly falls, peeling a layer of bark away from the trunk. He turns the saw off, hooks it by the handle to the 'beaner on his harness then loops the long rope around the tree's good fork, putting a running bowline on it.

He shakes the rope out for me, and I walk it away from the base of the tree to keep it free of his legs as he flip-lines and spurs his way down.

"Well," he says, once he's unhooked and standing next to me, "Looks like we can put the face-cut in right there and get it to lie down straight across the driveway."

I walk the guide rope across the asphalt. In my head we've already got this wood cut and piled at the curb for when G. L. and Rusty come by with the trailer.

"Relax," J. W. says climbing out of the harness and spurs, "Let's take five." I notice he's short of breath and sweating pretty hard, and I realize he hasn't been looking too good lately, like maybe he's got a bug or something. He stretches his arms and back as he walks over to the cooler to get a Gatorade.

"You're the boss," I say, letting the rope go, but part of me grinds. J. W.'s pissed about something; he's slowing us up on purpose, and I have no idea why.

"Something wrong?" I ask.

"Nah, there's nothing wrong." He opens the tailgate and sits down with his Gatorade. "Let's just relax a minute. This job isn't all about cut it down and drag it off, you know. Have a seat."

"That's alright," I say, "I don't wanna cramp up."

"Have it how you like," he says. He gets his pack of smokes from his shirt pocket, shakes one out and puts it to his lips, then he takes it away without lighting up and sits there holding the thing, looking at it like he's reading a thermometer.

"Mind if I bum one?" I ask.

He snaps back from wherever he's gone and eyes me up and down like I'm some dead tree, some snag, he's about to take out.

"Nasty habit," he says, and he holds out the smoke to me.

"That's why I do it," I say, grinning around the cigarette, "Got a light?"

"When you start smoking?" he asks.

I shrug.

"Your mom know you smoke?"

I shake my head no and take the lighter from him. I fire up the Camel, suck in a hard drag and hand the lighter back. The smoke tastes good. Carol Anne's already got me nearly hooked on her Winston Lights.

"There's a lot my mom doesn't know about me," I say.

Which is why I'm getting my own place. Why I want to finish this job and get on. Because I got things to do and bills to pay.

"Well, damn, if you ain't the big man." J. W. shakes a smoke from the pack for himself. "You oughta relax, Donny," he says, "You got a whole life to get through."

I smile and nod. What he doesn't know is that I'm already roaring down a dirt road toward the life he's talking about. I've got Carol Anne smashed up against me on the bench seat, her hand clamped on my thigh in a mix of terror and joy. I've got a smoke between the fingers of my one hand on the wheel, and the arm thrown across her shoulders ends with a beer in my fist. The radio is loud, I mean fucking LOUD, and we're laughing, screaming every time I top a hill because it seems like, fast as we're moving, we just might launch ourselves right out of here.

Goddamn kid is a good kid, but he's all crash and burn. These trees have a life he still hasn't learned to feel. And he wants to climb. Wants to work the saws. He's got to learn to know the tree before he can spur up, or that tree will sure as shit throw him down. He has to let the tree to show him where to cut, or that tree might make the saw take a finger, or his hand. He rolls his eyes when I try to tell him, acts like I'm talking some new age bullshit. If he didn't have pussy on the brain he'd listen when I say an arborist isn't about cut it up and pay me. An arborist is a surgeon, a healer, someone who cuts out what's dead or grown wrong so the rest can survive, flourish even. Sometimes the kid seems to get it. Sometimes, like today, like any Friday, it's nothing to him but a means to an end. A paycheck.

I stub out my smoke on the tailgate, shred what's left of the tobacco and stuff the butt in my pocket.

"Okay, Donny, let's do it," I tell him, and he walks the rope over to the other side of the driveway where he'll stand and pull once I put the back-cut in and the tree begins to lean. Usually I love this job, cutting away dead limbs and crossed branches and shaping a canopy away from rooftops and power lines, but this is just too much. Beverly told me when I did the bid that her husband doesn't have much time, and she needed get this handled right away because she doesn't want him staring out their front window at the wreckage of something he'd loved for so long. As if staring at the stump and the telephone pole behind it will be any better for him. The whole time she's telling me this, I can see some little girl behind her in the living room waiting on her accordion lesson, waiting to learn "Blow the Man Down" or "Greensleeves." Because that's what life does, it goes right on having accordion lessons in spite of us, and that's how Beverly keeps it together in the face of it all: she teaches the accordion to little kids and tries not to think about living without her husband. I charged her half of what I usually would, but she didn't even read the bid sheet—she would have paid whatever I asked. While she was signing I noticed all the school pictures and wedding pictures and baby pictures on the mantle behind her. They probably had sunny-day picnics with their kids and their grandkids horsing around in this yard in the shade of that tree, those sweet smelling clusters of honey locust flowers falling down around them like in some movie or a dream. Now the heart of that tree's been ripped open to the pulp and there's no saving it.

I crank up the Husky 450 and put in the face-cut, careful about the angle so the tree will lay itself down along the line I imagine.

"You ready," I shout over to Donny who looks to have his mind on what he'll be doing tonight with that girl instead of on what he's doing right now.

"Get your head out," I say, and he sets his mouth and nods, tightens his grip on the rope.

I'm three-quarters through the back-cut when the tree begins to lean wrong, falling toward my truck in slow motion, and I already see the bed crushed when Donny heaves on the guide-rope, barely managing to swing the trunk just past the trailer hitch so it's only branches scratching the truck and no real weight hitting the bed.

"Goddamn, Donny" I shout, cutting off the saw and running over. I've got to keep down the urge to smack him upside his head and knock off his hard hat.

"What happened? Weren't you pulling?" Then I notice he's just as upset as I am, and suddenly I'm not sure if it was his lack of pulling or my bad face cut that made the tree fall wrong.

"Hell yes, I was pulling," he says, "I was pulling my fucking ass off to keep it away from the bed. Why'd you face-cut like that? Why didn't you move the truck?"

I'm ready to tell him to shut his punk mouth because if fourteen years of tree work has taught me anything it's how to make a tree lie down where I want. Then I realize it could have been both our fault. Or neither. Trees will just fall their own way sometimes, no matter how much you know or how careful you are.

"Damn it, Donny. You got to pull harder," and I leave it at that, though I know he's right about how I just should've moved the truck in the first place. I look over my shoulder to check if Mr. Ashland has seen what's going on, but the picture window shade is down, and the house looks still and empty like he's already left us.

We start to section up the trunk and limbs, both of us catching ourselves now and then on the thorns. I let Donny work the little Husky, partly because I feel guilty for yelling at him, and partly because it's time he learns. He does good with the saw, uses it just like I showed him, as an extension of the line of his arm. Once we've finished, he grabs some of the choice cuts and starts setting them in the bed.

"Take those out," I say.

"Why?"

"Because I said so is why," I tell him, and I can see him bristle, but I don't care. Even if I tried to explain, he wouldn't understand the reasons why every single stick of it should stay here.

"I figured you wouldn't mind if I took some for tonight before G. L. and Rusty come with the trailer," he says.

"G. L. and Rusty got other things to do with the trailer," I say. "We're setting this wood up near the side door for Mr. Ashland. So get it out of the bed and don't fuck up his lawn starting the stack."

"Fine. Whatever," he says, taking the wood back out and setting it on the grass near the driveway. "You don't need to ream me out for it. I was just trying to score a little wood for the bonfire."

"Green wood don't do shit but hiss and smoke," I say.

"Well, since when do we stack people's wood for them."

"Since right now, goddammitt."

He lets out a groan to make sure I know he's pissed but still gathers up a big armload of logs and starts toward the side of the house. He is a strong kid, already bigger than a lot of men, and still without his full growth. He could become one mean, dangerous bastard if someone doesn't keep an eye on him. His mother has already sensed our old man's dark streak in him, and I owe it to her to do what I can. I shouldn't have snapped at him the way I did. Doesn't teach him much of anything worth learning.

It's three by time we've got all the honey locust stacked, the lawn around the stump raked, and the sawdust swept off the driveway and walk. I don't bother knocking to tell Mr. Ashland we're through; if he's resting, he doesn't need to be disturbed, and Beverly and me have already discussed the check I'll be getting in the mail. So I just pull the carbon off the paperwork, fold it up, and stick it in the mailbox mounted next to the front door of the house.

Donny's already in my truck waiting when I come down the walk. I can tell through the windshield that he's searching my eyes, trying to see if I'm still pissed at him or if I'm just tired. Well, I am tired, all the time lately, and irritable, and this weird itch in my throat makes me think I should go see a doctor even though I don't want to. Maybe I'm just getting old. Only thirty-three, and I can't climb and carry quite like I used to, though I've learned some little thing with each tree I've taken down. Each tree that is so much more than a tree if you take the time to understand what you're dealing with and why.

"That's all for today," I say as I get in and slam the door, "Let's knock off."

"Knock off?" Donny doesn't try to hide the disappointment in his voice. "You sure?"

"Yes, I'm sure," I say, "And yeah you'll be getting your pay in cash today so quit your bitching."

"I wasn't bitching."

I take a smoke out and light it, thumb without looking over to the stump I've cut nearly level with the ground. "Donny, what kind of tree was that we just took out?"

"I don't know. A linden?"

"A honey locust, Donny. Some of the hardest wood there is next to ebony. Tree like that can live a hundred and fifty years or more, see generations of people come and go unless some storm or sickness takes it down."

"Not this one."

His smartass shit nearly makes me snap, but I can't blame him. He doesn't realize anything more than he's sore and swiping back at me. I take a deep breath, calm myself. I don't want to drop the ball this time.

"That's not the point," I say. "Point is you need to learn the difference between the trees, Donny. It's important to know the differences when most people see things as the same."

"Okay," he says, flatly, "I'll get to work on that," and I decide to take what he says in a good way.

"Can I bum another smoke?"

I turn the engine over, toss my pack into his lap, "From now on you start buying your own."

I back out of the driveway and pull onto the street in front of Mr. Ashland's house. Before I drop it into Drive, I look across Donny at the pale green ranch. Mr. Ashland is there at the stump, down on one knee, an unlit cigarette between his lips. He's running his fingers lightly over my cut, following the rings in a slow circle. I imagine he's considering time. All that has passed. How much he has left. There is the honey locust wood stacked against the side of his house. A year, at least, before it will be dry enough to burn, and I doubt he even has that long.

Already, I can feel the absence of my half-nephew next to me. He's gone, off in his mind thinking about a future of drinking cheap beer with his buddies and their girlfriends beside a hissing, smoky bonfire at the lake. I consider tapping the horn to get Mr. Ashland's attention so I can wave goodbye, but I don't because he lifts his head just then as if called. He's looking right at me, though I can tell it isn't really me he's looking at. It's something else, something that makes him smile. And that's what he's doing as I smile back and drive away: smiling a tight, grim smile, his fingers still circling and working their way toward the center of that tree's severed life where he will end by touching the beginning.